GW01539766

To my dear ... a sweet and ...

R♡

The Spirit Within

Rikki

Bright Pen

Visit us online at www.authorsonline.co.uk

A Bright Pen Book

ISBN 0 7552 1022 0

Authors OnLine Ltd
40 Castle Street
Hertford SG14 1HR
England

This book is also available in e-book format, details of
which are available at www.authorsonline.co.uk

Acknowledgements

It is difficult to know where to begin to acknowledge those who have made it possible for this story to be written and published, for my life has been a journey of interconnected pieces, all of which have led me to this place.

I have been blessed with a group of friends and family members who have shown me unending love and support. I've had a fabulous cheerleading team behind me, helping me in so many different ways, seeing me through dark times, and delighting in my successes. They have encouraged me to be all that I am meant to be, and to follow my dreams. To begin to list each of these special people and all they have given me would require a whole other book! You and I know who you are, though, and I offer all of you my appreciation, my love, and my gratitude.

Mom, you've always been very supportive of my 'artistic abilities', whether it's with my music, my art or my writing. You always said I should be a writer, so I was a good kid and did as I was told!! Thank you for all your encouragement and I hope this makes you proud.

Dad, I wish you could be here to share this with me. You were always one of my biggest fans and supporters, and although I know you're still watching from 'the other side', it's not the same as having you 'here'. You always told me I could do or be anything I wanted, and now, I'm living out one of my dreams. Thank you for having been such a great father. I miss you...

Reg, you are the most amazing husband who ever lived. I am the envy of many women who wish they were in my shoes! (well, sandals! We know how allergic I am to shoes!) You are so patient and kind, so loving and thoughtful. You put up with my various quirks, and you have fulfilled so many of my dreams! You feed my soul and I only wish I could tell you how much I love and appreciate you.

Charles, thank you for all the time and effort you spent on putting this book together, and also for doing without your lovely wife during her tireless hours working on my behalf so that this book could be published.

And then there is Pat Senior, of Authors Incorporated. Pat, you truly are an Angel who has been sent to me, changing my life in the most incredible ways... I'm supposed to be a writer, but I am really stuck for words. You have opened up a whole new world to me, and have given me more gifts of love than I could ever have imagined one person could give another. Not only have I found a wonderful publisher, I have found a beautiful friend. I can't begin to thank you for all you have done for me. There simply are no words, but my heart overflows with love and appreciation for you.

I am very grateful to 'The Universe' for these many gifts of loving relationships, and for the Divine spark within me, which together have allowed me to create this book.

About the Author

To say that Rikki is quirky is something of an understatement. Her favourite expression is that she lives so far outside the box, she can't see it any more. Some of her very favourite things are old doors, creaky things, bare feet, the moon, old stuff that's falling apart, and creating conversations in silly voices for animals, insects, and anybody else she happens to find in nature.

She finds the greatest of pleasures in some of the simplest of things, like giggling, covering her living room ceiling in years' worth of her children's art work, bad puns, red peppers, misty days, listening to a howling wind, and her very favourite music played loudly enough to burst the neighbour's eardrums.

Growing up in Calgary, Alberta, Canada, near the Rocky Mountains which she loves and misses, Rikki was a shy and very sensitive child who loved to draw, to write, and to play the organ and piano. To meet her now, you would be surprised to imagine that someone with such an enthusiasm for life could have possibly been so shy!

As she grew, she acknowledged that although each of us is a unique individual, she felt different in an unexplainable manner. It was as though she did not belong anywhere. It took years of unhappily trying to 'fit in' before Rikki realized that it was okay to be herself, and to be 'different'.

And that's when the fun began! Rikki has always been a Seeker, exploring the depths of herself and her soul, searching for meaning in all things, yearning for deeper understanding of herself, others, the world, the Universe, and especially, all 'Things Spiritual'.

Her many health issues led her on a different kind of

search, a search for true healing, which she found in homeopathy. She was so impressed with the power of this remarkable science, that after many years as a counsellor and hypnotist, she began a course of study, ultimately graduating from The Devon School of Homeopathy in England. This education, combined with her life experiences and her natural healing abilities, allow her to be a very successful homeopath. It always gives her great pleasure when the Universe sends her someone she is meant to heal, as she well knows how it feels when suffering stops.

Rikki well remembers her serious illness, and values every moment of every day, believing that as each second passes, all those remaining become increasingly valuable. She entirely understands and accepts her own mortality, having stared Death in the face on countless occasions, and therefore, she works hard to make the best choices she can in everything she says or does.

Wayne Dyer asserts that we are not human beings having a spiritual experience; we are spiritual beings having a human experience. Rikki believes this to be so, and strives to live her life based on these words.

Currently, she resides in a quaint 1700s stone cottage that is about as quirky as she is. It is located in a tiny village in England, a couple of minutes' walk from a lovely little lake. Rikki loves to go there; she says it feeds her soul. In her life, she has loved walking, cooking, target shooting with handguns, gardening, travel, communicating, painting (murals and abstract art being her favourites, see www.artbyrivkah.com), sketching, decorating, and numerous other activities. She values respect, responsibility and honesty, and most of all, she is passionate about every moment of this Life.

Contents

I Am Devoured

In February of 2004, a lifetime of stress, crises and coping finally beat me and I broke. Already having been a person who was very much interested in healing and spirituality, though the rest of that year was one of the worst I had ever had, that also made it one of the best. I was forced to dismantle myself and every belief I ever had, and dig even deeper than ever in my search for healing.

In the early days of that very dark time, however, I felt as though I was being eaten alive by a nightmare. I had fallen into a deep black hole, so far that I could not see the light at the top any more, and I thought I might never get out.

This very short piece came from that time.

I Am Devoured

It waits. It creates the darkness as bait for tormented souls, whose obsession with it will entice. Then it lurks, silently, patiently, waiting to feed on its prey. I leave the light and enter its shadows. It is hiding there, still, as its ominous intentions creep forth, billowing and unstoppable.

I seem to have no will of my own. I am drawn to the shadows as I approach, my back to the light which grows dimmer with each of my hesitant steps, and fades imperceptibly, and now I am in blackness, though how it happened eludes me. It seems I must have always been surrounded by it; I no longer remember the light, which so quietly disappeared without my notice.

And in the blackness which it created, I know it is there, though I can't see it. I can almost hear it, a long, low rumbling, growling, or can I just feel it? Certainly, its presence is undeniable, unmistakable. To find oneself in its company is to become the prey, to know that survival is questionable. Doubtful. The predator is unrelenting, ceaseless in its desire for satisfaction.

I am captured. I am the hostage. I am bound. I am in chains. I cannot move. I am immobilized. And still it waits. It taunts and torments me; it teases me with glimpses of freedom in the light, and I think I may taste it again, as it relaxes its crushing grip. But freedom is mine no more. No, not even a taste, not a morsel. I am once again plunged into the darkness, where it delights in my terror, which amuses it so. It toys with me, contemplating whether to devour me, or to push me into the quicksand.

If its decision is to devour me, I wonder whether it will be with a gluttonous fervour, ripping and tearing, grunting in hedonistic pleasure as it tastes my blood, or whether it will be as a sensitive lover, teasing and tantalizing with strawberries, dangling each one just above full and slightly parted lips, the tongue delicately licking at them, darting in and out of the mouth, tasting the juices. And after a time, unhurriedly biting into the fruit, sensuously savouring each bit of its flesh, until the leisurely meal is swallowed in its entirety.

And if its decision is the push into the quicksand, it will take great pleasure in watching me struggle, it will delight in my desperation, and with every movement, I shall sink deeper still, until I am unable to move. The onslaught will be merciless as it violates and invades me, pushing its way past my nose, my mouth, my throat, forcing me to devour my own death.

I can do nothing but wait...wait in the black terror...wait to see whether my captor will release me...wait to see whether I am devoured, whether I will live or die...wait for the light, and wonder, hopelessly, if it will ever come...

The Greedy Artist's Awakening

It is said that all of our choices and behaviours come from one of two very powerful forces: love or fear. This is the story of a man who is driven by the very destructive power of fear.

The Greedy Artist's Awakening

Once upon a time, there was a little boy who loved to paint. He was not very good at it, but no one could bear to tell him so. He lived in a cramped little house with his mother and father, and the three barely had room to turn around. The boy's father had been ill for some time, and could not manage much by way of work. The mother took in laundry, and tried to get some work cleaning other homes, but there was not much of it to be had.

And so they struggled along, doing their best to make ends meet. There was very little food much of the time, and even less variety. Many times, a meal was a small portion of rice or a potato, but somehow, they carried on. Sometimes, there were vegetables from his mother's garden, when they had been able to obtain seeds and plant them. But then, much depended upon the weather conditions, and the seeds did not always yield much for all the effort that had gone into the garden. And meat, oh, my goodness. What a treat, when his parents could scrape together a few coins to buy a small amount of it, or when kind neighbours shared theirs. It broke his parents' hearts that they could not provide more for their son, but they loved him more than anything, and did their very best for him in difficult circumstances.

The boy hated such poverty, and swore that he would one day become a rich and very famous artist. He hated living with the fear that there would not be enough food, or that the family's home would be taken from them. He wanted to be able to buy absolutely anything and everything his heart desired, and still have enough money left over to do it a million times more. But how would he ever get to be a rich and famous artist, if he could not afford the supplies to practice painting? Frustration simmered through the boy, sometimes reaching a boiling anger, and once in a while, it was again reduced to a slow simmer when a kind neighbour would bring him a few bits of paint or canvas. When he was old enough to begin doing odd jobs for villagers, he was a little happier, as he was better able to keep himself in art supplies. It never occurred to him to offer any of his money to his parents to help them buy food or pay for other necessities; he thought only about his painting. His parents understood how he felt about his art work, and so they never asked him to contribute any of his earnings so that they could buy more food. Rather, they continued to do their best with what they had, and encouraged him to pursue his dream.

One spring day, it was announced at school that there would be an art contest. The boy was certain that he would win because he believed himself to be a far better artist than he actually was. If the truth be told, he was covering deep feelings of inadequacy, brought on by his impoverished life. He covered these feelings so well that even he, himself, was unaware of them. Instead, he simply felt fear whenever he thought about money, and every time he painted, he believed himself to be one step closer to his dream of being rich and famous, reducing his anxiety a little. To him, winning this contest was a giant leap in that direction.

Excitedly, he laboured over the painting that he intended to enter, painstakingly creating what he was certain to be the winning masterpiece. And when he had finished, he stood back from his easel, admiring his work. Closing his eyes, he could hear the crowds cheering, and the judges saying that there was no point in anyone else having entered because he was so obviously the winner.

Such daydreams gave the boy a bit of relief from his lonely

life of poverty. They sustained him and gave him a goal, upon which he focused constantly. He often thought about how people pitied him, and how he detested the sad looks on their faces. Eagerly, he awaited the day when he would instead see looks of envy, as they admired his fame and his wealth.

From the day that the contest was announced, the boy spoke long and often with his parents about it, stating with absolute certainty that he would win. They were very supportive of the boy's efforts, and always wished him well. He could not wait to bring home the big blue ribbon; it would make him feel as though he had taken the first serious step toward achieving his goal of having fame and fortune, and it would make him feel less like he was part of a pitied, poverty-stricken family. His parents would be so proud, and heaven knew they did not have much of anything else that could give them a sense of pride.

Finally, the big day arrived. The boy carried his painting ever so carefully, all the way from home, anticipating the moment when the cloth would be removed, and there would be gasps of astonishment as all in attendance gazed upon his impressive work.

All the contestants were gathered together in the gymnasium, and each student stood beside an easel, upon which his or her painting rested, covered. When everyone was ready, the judges, teachers and parents were called in for the unveiling. The boy was filled with excitement when the contestants were finally told to uncover their work.

As paintings were exposed, there were oohs and aaahs from the crowd, along with quiet whispers and low voices describing the beauty they beheld. Of course, the boy was certain that everyone was speaking about his masterpiece, and he stood, chest thrust forward, beaming.

It took some time for the judges to wander amongst the contestants, staring intently at each work of art, making notes, going back to some of them a few times. On occasion, the judges peered very closely at a painting, eyes squinting.

The boy decided that they must be trying to make the other contestants feel like they were really getting a fair chance at winning, since they already knew who would come away with the blue ribbon, and would not want to offend the other children. He waited patiently for the moment that they announced him as the winner.

It took some time for the judges to finish their examinations of all work that had been entered in the contest, and then they spent some time chatting amongst themselves, looking at their notes, pointing at the paintings. The boy knew that this was all for show, 'Although,' he thought, 'they do need to choose second and third place as well. That must be what all the discussion is about.

Finally, one of the judges stepped forward, and stood at a microphone in the center of the crowd. Clearing his throat, he began a short but moving speech about the talent and the effort that had been put forth by the contestants. Of course, he made the usual sort of statements to do with achieving goals, and with being proud of one's accomplishments. He said that they could not all win the contest, but told them that each was a winner in his or her own way. He also spoke of choosing a winner having been such a difficult choice. The boy knew that the judge was just being polite, but he appreciated that it would be nice for those who did not win to hear such kind words.

A smug smile hung on the boy's face as the judge went on

to announce the child who had taken third place. The crowd applauded, and there were a few whistles, as the happy child went up to receive his ribbon, the applause subsiding as he walked back to his painting.

It was the same as the judge called the name of the second place winner, a rather chubby little girl who seemed not to do anything but smile any day of the week, which the boy had always found to be most annoying.

And there it was; his long-awaited moment of recognition and glory. The judge waited for the crowd to settle after the smiling girl went back to her place before he began to speak.

"And in first place," he said, as the boy began to move toward him, "Sheila Pinkham!!"

The stunned boy stopped dead in his tracks, the smug smile immediately replaced by a look of shock. He felt sick and hot, as his face flushed with embarrassment, since many people had seen him begin to walk toward the judges, expecting that he had won. He was grateful that all eyes were on Sheila at that moment, and his faux pas was quickly forgotten. Embarrassment soon gave way to outrage, as he listened to the applause that should have been for him. It seemed that everything was suddenly moving in slow motion, as the blood rushed past his ears, and the sounds of the cheering crowds were swallowed by his rage.

He turned and ran as fast as his legs would carry him. He did not know where he was going, nor did he care. He just had to run. And before long, the tears streaming down his face, he had put quite a bit of distance between himself and those horribly stupid judges. He wanted to leave the feelings of inadequacy behind as well, but when he finally stopped running, panting hard and falling to the ground, he found that they had followed him. And he knew in that moment that they would be with him wherever he went, until he was very famous and very rich.

The boy lay there for a long time, in the middle of an empty field, where no one could see him, or hear his heartbroken sobbing. He cried until he could cry no longer, tears of hurt, of frustration and jealousy. And what made the whole situation worse was how awful he thought Sheila Pinkham was to begin with! She was a scrawny, pale, whiney little thing, with lots of allergies, and she was always sniffling and blowing her nose. She was about the most annoying girl in the whole school! How on earth could those judges pick her over him? And that painting that they thought was so wonderful -- hah! He had more artistic ability in his little finger than she would ever have in a lifetime. Those judges obviously had no idea what they were doing, and they certainly were not qualified for the job. The more he thought about the entire issue, the more disgusted he became.

His shame and humiliation fed his anger and jealousy, mighty beasts that they were becoming. They grew inside him like a fire raging out of control, and before long, he was able to pick himself up and slowly make his way home. By then, it was getting dark. His parents had been very worried about him, and he struggled to tell them what had happened. He had been so certain he would win, and it made him sick to think that he had to come home without any ribbon at all.

Of course, his parents were not concerned about whether or not he had won, they loved him just the same. But they well understood how terribly disappointed and upset their son was feeling. They tried, unsuccessfully, to console him. There was nothing they could say that even slightly diminished his rage or his shame.

He was very quiet that evening, and for a long time afterward. He seemed to have retreated into himself completely, and began to work harder at finding odd jobs, in order to buy more paints and canvas. Every penny he earned went toward art supplies, and he became driven in a way his parents had never seen before. When he was not working at earning money, he was working on his paintings. He began to sleep very little, determined to create art that was going to make him rich beyond his wildest imaginings.

When he did sleep, he was always restless, thrashing around in his small bed, becoming tangled in the sheets. He began to have one particular dream with great regularity, a dream that he could never quite remember, but one that always caused him to wake with a start, drenched in sweat. All he could ever remember of this dream was that it was very dark, and there was an eerie figure that seemed to be beckoning, calling to him, with a bony, claw-like hand that stretched out to him from the folds of a long, black cloak. There were never any words spoken, and he could not make out the face, but there was no mistaking the feeling in this dream. It was very ominous, terrifying, and felt very, very real. And the worst part was that this dream occurred very frequently for many long years.

His parents became worried about their pale and exhausted son, but every attempt to express their concern was met with an angry retort, and the boy would storm off to his room, slamming the door behind him as he headed for his paints.

The years passed and the boy's parents died. His father had not seen the boy reach adulthood, his health having been poor for much of the child's life. His mother finally succumbed to disease caused by poverty. The strain of such worry, and an inadequate diet finally took their toll. And when she died, the boy, then a young man, sold the family's home and moved to a run-down little cottage at the edge of a remote and tiny village. In doing so, he was able to save most of the money he received from the sale of the house, and he could devote his days to his beloved painting. He was happy to have a little nest egg, but he was certain that he would make a good living, selling his paintings in this new village. Soon, word would spread of this great artist's creations, and people would be flocking to him from miles around. He needed to be ready with a good supply, so he set to work, painting day and night.

It was not often that anyone passed by his cottage, due to the location, and the fact that there were not many people in the village anyway. But when anyone did happen along the path on a sunny day, the artist could be seen in the garden, busily creating his paintings. When it rained, he moved himself indoors and continued. He had heard about some very famous artists whose work was selling for loads and loads of money, and he wanted to be counted amongst them. And so he barely ate or slept, so he could paint and paint and paint. Unfortunately, the paintings were still of a very poor quality, but the artist could not see it.

Many times, people who passed by called out a word of greeting to the artist. If he replied at all, it was without looking up from his work, and it was more of a growl than anything. Occasionally, someone would try to strike up a friendly conversation, or ask if he would like to visit them for a cup of tea, but he would turn them away, gruffly telling them that he could not be bothered, and saying that he was busy creating masterpieces which would make him rich and famous. To him, friends were a waste of his valuable creating time.

On occasion, there would be a knock at the door, with someone on the other side of it needing his help. And on every occasion, he would bark through the closed door, "Go away!" irritated that anyone would interrupt his creative process. 'My goodness,' he would think to himself. 'How am I ever going to become rich and famous with all these people bothering me?!' And he would turn his attention back to his creations.

After a while, people stopped calling to him as they passed, and there were no more offers of friendship. And most certainly, no one came looking for help. The artist had finally made it clear that he wanted nothing to do with any of the villagers.

In time, his little cottage was bursting at the seams, for it could no longer contain all of his paintings. He could not understand why no one would buy them; after all, they were so beautiful! He puzzled over this very many times. The people in the village knew he was a very busy artist; they saw him outside painting often enough. So why, then, did no one stop in to have a look and take one home, leaving lots of their money in his hands? Becoming quite disgusted with the stupidity of the villagers, his frustration and anger grew, along with his ever-increasing desire to be rich and famous.

There he was, with a vast collection of his art, and it was not moving. Still, he continued to buy lots of paints and many rolls of canvas, and he kept creating. His nest egg began to dwindle, as he had not yet begun to earn anything from what he believed to be his God-given talent and destiny.

Eventually, the man was just about out of money. His plan had gone awry. He had long since begun eating very little, trying to make his money last as long as possible. When it came down to a choice between food and art supplies, he opted for very little food, determined to have the best possible selection of paintings for his customers to view. He was certain that one day soon, that first buyer was going to knock on his door, and he needed to be ready for the swarms of people whom he was sure would follow. With such a poor diet, and with only a tiny bit of rest each night, it was not long before his health began to fail. Always a very miserly man, as the money in his jar dwindled, he became even more fearful and obsessed with having enough to support several kingdoms.

Late one stormy evening, the man was busily painting yet another picture by the light of one lonely little candle. Lightning flashed, illuminating the night sky, while deafening cracks of thunder fairly shook the little cottage. He barely seemed to notice the raging storm, in all likelihood because it matched his mood. As the wind howled, and whistled through the cracks in the cottage, he suddenly had the strangest sensation that he was not alone. He felt as though he was being watched, and the hairs on the back of his neck stood straight up.

He stopped painting, listening intently, afraid to move. Fear gripped his heart, as he grew certain that there was, indeed, someone there with him. Swallowing hard, his throat suddenly very dry, he slowly turned around. As he scanned the darkened room, his stomach churned and seemed to drop to his knees when there, in the shadows, he saw the vague outline of a cloaked figure.

He choked back a scream that he was certain would have been blood-curdling, had it escaped from his tight, dry throat. It could not be! This was his nightmare, come to life! Terror filled every part of his being, from every cell of his body, straight through to the center of his soul.

Struggling unsuccessfully to hide his fear, the deep and intimidating voice for which he had been searching was, instead, tight and thin, as he barked, "Who are you? What do you want?!"

Silence was the only reply.

"How did you get in? I'm warning you, get out of here immediately!" His terror was unmistakable; all efforts to mask it were futile.

The figure moved slightly, but toward him and out of the shadows just a little; there was no evidence of an impending retreat. He had not thought it possible to be any more terrified than he had already been, but this little movement proved him to be wrong. The artist's terror continued to grow, as he seemed be not at all threatening to this intruder, whose eerie presence caused his blood to run cold, chilling him to the bone.

The only sounds the artist could now hear were his own heart pounding in his chest, and the blood rushing past his ears. Once again, the figure edged a little closer to him, and he heard the quiet rustle of the cloak, swishing across the floor. Still, not a word from his unwelcome guest, who slowly moved closer and into the dim light of the flickering candle.

The artist's heart was beating wildly, and his breath was shallow and ragged. His mind was racing, as he struggled to find a way to end this nightmare.

And then, the figure stepped forward, moving out of the shadows. The artist saw an ugly, old woman, the hood of her black cloak loosely covering long, stringy, gray strands of hair. Her face, contorted and terrifying, was the colour of Death.

"What do you want from me?" the artist demanded, his mouth as dry as the desert sand at mid-day.

The crone was silent for a moment. And when she began to speak, the hair on the back of the artist's neck once again stood on end, her low and raspy voice causing him to shudder.

"I have come to give you all you have worked for, to see that you get exactly what you have earned."

The man was puzzled. All he had worked for? Fame and fortune were all he wanted, but how could this terrifying and broken old crone give him these?

"Wh-wh-what do you mean?" he stammered in confusion and fear.

"I mean exactly what I said. I have come to grant your wishes," was the quiet reply, that horrible voice making the man shudder.

The artist's fear began to leave him, as thoughts and images of wealth and notoriety flooded into his mind.

"And how will you do that?" he asked, suspicious of her statements.

"You will see. But first, you must promise that one day, you will do something for me."

The man thought for a moment, suddenly not quite as excited about the proposition. After all, he did not much care for doing anything for another.

"And just what is it that you would have me do?" he queried, somewhat defiantly.

"That remains to be seen. It will be one request, one time, but I know not what it will be, or when I will ask. In return, you will have fame and wealth beyond your wildest imaginings, just as you have always desired."

The man pondered the crone's words for a few moments. His money was about to run out, it was true, and certainly, he was not selling any of his paintings, though he could not understand why. He decided that with fame and fortune, he would have enough people working for him, and enough money behind him, that anything the old woman could ever ask in the future would be easily managed, so it seemed a fair exchange.

"All right," he said firmly. "I will agree to your terms."

At that moment, a little draft seemed to rush past the back of the man's neck, causing a chill which he found somewhat disconcerting.

The crone reached deep into a black, drawstring bag, and pulled out a glass bottle with an old cork stuffed in its neck. With her bony hand, she held it out to the man, and he vividly recalled the claw-like fingers in his dream.

"What's this?" he asked, reaching hesitantly for it.

"It is a Transformation Potion," the old woman replied. "Put a drop on yourself and you will be seen as the most gifted artist who ever lived. Then put a drop on each of your paintings, and they will be seen as beautiful works of art that no one will be able to resist, no matter what the cost."

The man was most insulted by these remarks. His hand shot back from the bottle. "How dare you, Old Woman?!" he exclaimed, with great indignation. "I *am* a very gifted artist, and my paintings *are* beautiful works of art!"

"You are wrong, sir, on both counts, but I am not here to argue either point. Simply do as I tell you, and very soon, you will receive all you deserve. And remember our agreement. One day, I shall return to make a request of you, and you shall do as I ask."

Offended, yet eager for his wishes to be granted, the man decided to let the crone's comments pass without further debate. It was more important for him to have all the money he could possibly imagine, than it was for him to convince her that she was wrong.

With a look on his face which bordered on disgust, the artist snatched the bottle out of the old woman's gnarled hand. Turning his attention to it, and staring at the glass, he wondered how soon he would be rich. He looked up to ask the crone this question, but she had vanished without a sound.

That night, the artist did not sleep. Instead, he thrashed around in his bed as he contemplated his future, eager to be wealthy and famous. As the sun rose, it found him out of his bed, having a very early start to his day, eager to reap the rewards of all his hard work. With the daylight, he was better able to reach all of his paintings, stacked and buried in his cottage, and put a drop of the transformation potion on each.

Once he had completed his task, he carefully put a drop on himself. He felt a tingle run through his body, like a little electrical charge. It disappeared after a few moments, and the artist was somewhat disappointed when he did not notice any other changes. He hoped that he had not been duped, and was readying himself to find the old crone and have it out with her if nothing came of this.

18

He did not have to wait long, however, to see that she had been true to her word. Before most people would have even sat down to breakfast, there were knocks upon the door, with people on the other side, asking if they could please see his paintings. He was all smiles, as he waved them in, and, oh, how he delighted in hearing them oooh and aaaah at his creations.

Over the following days, his previously bulging little cottage was rapidly being emptied, as more and more people came, anxious to purchase his paintings. They could not seem to buy them quickly enough, so the greedy artist began to raise the prices. It almost seemed as though the more the paintings cost, the faster they were sold.

The more they bought, the faster he raised the prices. The cost did not seem to matter to them; they had to have his paintings, just as the crone had told him it would be. Some were even heard discussing how it was going to create serious financial hardship for them, yet they seemed driven to purchase his paintings, despite the consequences. He did not seem to notice that these people were using their food money, and lots of it, to buy his art. Rather, as he listened to those discussions, all he gathered was that he must be an amazing artist to cause people to go to such lengths to own one of his paintings.

Soon, all his paintings were gone, and he had several large sacks of money hidden under his bed. He simply could not believe his eyes! Finally, he was able to purchase more art supplies, and better ones, and he set about the business of creating many more paintings, turning away countless disappointed people, who promised they would return when he had replenished his supply.

It did not take long before the artist was, indeed, very famous and very wealthy. News of his incredible talent and paintings spread like wildfire, and soon, the man had moved to a beautiful castle, high on a hill, overlooking the sea. He had more servants than he could possibly ever need, many of whom had no real work to do, but the artist enjoyed being able to tell everyone how many he required. It seemed to impress people, and it added to his feelings of importance and superiority.

Though the man already had far more money than he could ever use, his greed and ambition did not diminish. In fact, they seemed to grow. The more money he had, the more he believed he needed to have. Day and night, he continued to paint, barely stopping to eat. He was still putting increasingly ridiculous prices on his paintings, along with a little of the Transformation Potion, of course, and people who could ill afford them still flocked to his castle, putting themselves into dire financial straits just to own his creations. The artist would only laugh and rub his hands together with glee when he saw them coming, and was even more excited about taking all their money before they left.

One day, the artist was on a castle balcony, painting the ocean view from his lofty position. It was a lovely, sunny day, and the water was a particularly brilliant shade of blue. He loved listening to the waves, crashing into the shore, amidst the cries of the gulls as they swooped and soared overhead. A delicate breeze played with the leaves on the trees, creating a soft, rustling sound, which was somewhat soothing to the man who lived with constant anxiety. It was the first time he could remember feeling any sort of love or appreciation for the beauty around him. Though it was a strange feeling, it warmed his heart, and gave him a sense of peace that was entirely unfamiliar to him.

As he stared out at the lovely scene below him, he noticed in the distance a young woman, walking alone along the cliffs. Curious about her, he stopped painting, holding his brush in mid-air, and he watched. Her movements were unhurried, and she paused frequently to look out over the water for a few moments before walking a little further.

Eventually, she climbed up on a rather large rock, and seated herself so that she was facing the ocean. The sea breeze played with her long, flowing hair, and holding her face to the sun, she leaned back on her hands, feet dangling high above the water.

The artist was smitten, though he could not even see the woman clearly. She was near enough for him to know that she was very beautiful, but too far away to be seen distinctly. He sat, mesmerized for some time.

Suddenly, he found himself leaving his paints and brushes, and dashing through the castle halls, tearing down stairways, and racing across the grounds. Once on the other side of the wall, he hurried along the shore of the ocean, until he had the woman in his sight. Composing himself, he ran his fingers through his hair, straightened his clothes, and forced himself to hide his nervousness as he sauntered toward her, a slight stagger in his gait, as he overcompensated for his anxiety by trying extra hard to look as though he were quite confident.

The woman had not moved in some time. She was still sitting on the rock, leaning back on her hands, face to the sun, when he had got within several feet of her. He could see that her eyes were closed, but he was certain that she should have been able to hear him approaching on the rocks, yet she seemed unaware of his presence.

He faltered, wondering whether he should interrupt her obvious deep thoughts, wondering whether he was intruding, wondering whether he should turn back and run from her. He had no experience with women, having been consumed by his burning need to paint and become wealthy, so he was entirely lost.

As he stood in his place, staring at the beauty before him, and wondering what he should next do, he was startled when the woman suddenly spoke. Without opening her eyes or moving, she simply said, "Come, sit here beside me."

The artist was more than a little surprised by this; she had not even seen the person who had intruded on her peaceful afternoon. Without a word, he climbed up on the rock, and then hesitated, wondering just how much distance he should leave between himself and the woman.

"Right beside me," she directed, as though she had read his thoughts. It was more than a little strange, and was somewhat disconcerting, yet he did not question her, and instead, he merely complied.

"You live in the castle," she stated; she was not asking.

Once again, the artist felt a little uncomfortable with her manner, but simply responded, "Yes, I do. How did you know?"

She laughed, tossing her head back, and then turned to him, finally opening her eyes and looking at the man she had invited to sit beside her. "You are famous and wealthy. I know more about you than you would believe."

"Ah," he said, feeling a little more comfortable, having got a reason for her having this knowledge, while at the same time, a little more disconcerted, wondering just exactly how much she knew. He felt almost as though he were unclothed, as if she could see right through him, and he worried about what she might find.

The two sat and talked for a while, she in her wisdom, he in his nervousness, and after a time, he felt brave enough to invite her to the castle for a drink and a meal. She was only too happy to agree, which surprised and delighted the artist, and they walked back together as the sun was beginning to sink into the ocean.

After the two had shared a lovely meal that evening, the artist took the woman to his studio, and showed her his paintings. Having used the Transformation Potion for so long, he was used to people being extremely impressed with his work, and he had forgotten that it was the potion that created this reaction, and not actually his art. As they walked through the open door, they were immediately faced with numerous paintings hanging on the walls, or standing on easels. The artist's face was filled with pride, waiting for the usual reaction that he got from viewers.

But this time it was different. The woman did not say much about any of them, nor did she seem particularly impressed. She wore a rather bored expression, and seemed to be attempting to be polite in her reactions. He was puzzled by this, to be sure. He had not seen anything like it since he got his magical potion years before.

The artist felt panic arising from his stomach. What if the potion was wearing off? What if no one wanted to see his work any more? What if he never sold another painting? Yes, it was true that he had a ridiculous amount of money, but he believed that one could never have too much, and he was not at all prepared to stop earning it already!

As for the woman's opinion, it did not particularly matter to him what she thought of his work, except in the context of worrying that the potion was no longer working. He was so smitten with her, that he would not have cared if she said she detested everything he created.

Hiding his concerns about the potion and the money, he continued to have a wonderful evening with the woman, until it was time for her to take her leave. He called for a servant to prepare a coach and horses, and the two waited outside in the cool summer air for the driver to appear. Riding together in the carriage, both spoke of how they had enjoyed the evening. It was a sweet parting that evening, both the artist and the woman expressing their desire to see each other again soon. On the way home, the man simply could not believe his good fortune. This woman seemed to touch a part of his soul that he had not known existed, and it was wonderful.

They spent a lot of time together in the weeks that followed; the artist was somewhat relieved to have a break from his round-the-clock painting, which had become a lifestyle. His anxiety about money had not dissipated by any means, but he was enjoying this wonderful new relationship so much that it distracted him from worrying excessively. Not wanting to face the issue of the potion, and the possibility of not selling any more paintings, he stopped allowing customers in, saying he was on holiday. In this way, he was not only able to quiet his fears to a great extent, he was also able to better enjoy the time he spent with the woman.

It did not take the artist long to work up the courage to propose marriage to her one night, over a beautiful, candlelit dinner on the balcony, overlooking the last remnants of a striking sunset, so stunningly reflected in the sea.

For all the confidence he had with his paintings, he certainly had none with women, since this was all new to him. Really, he thought himself quite bold to dare to ask such a lovely young woman for her hand in marriage. Deep in his heart, he did not believe that he deserved such a wife, but he certainly would not want to admit this to anyone, not with his position in society! How delighted he was, when she happily agreed to become his wife.

Because of his ongoing anxiety about money, he was rather afraid to bring up the subject of their wedding. He was torn between wanting to have a very lavish one, if that was what she wanted, and a simple and inexpensive celebration, knowing that the potion may not be working any longer, thereby cutting off his ability to earn any money. He was very happy, however, when she broached the subject with him, telling him that she was hoping he would not mind, but she really wanted a very private, quiet affair.

It was another of those disconcerting moments for the artist; he felt as though she had read his mind. He wondered briefly if he would ever get used to that, then brushed off the feeling that it elicited, and chose, instead, to return to the matter at hand. He tried to hide his relief about her decision, but did the polite and appropriate thing, asking her if she was absolutely certain. "After all, my love," he said, "This will be your only wedding, and it must be as you wish."

She smiled and nodded gently, reassuring him that it was, in fact, as she wished.

They did not waste any time in seeing to the simple arrangements, and before long, they were standing together on the rock where they met by the sea, proclaiming their love for one another, and becoming husband and wife. It was a magical day; the artist seemed to forget his worries and his ambitions for much of it, and he simply delighted in the joy of having this lovely young woman become his wife.

It was the happiest day of his life. In fact, when he looked back over his years right through to childhood, he realized that he had never known happiness until he met her.

The two seemed well-suited to each other; he was not much of a conversationalist, never having spent much time around people, and she was very quiet. Both seemed content with the long silences between them. They simply enjoyed being together. He soon began to paint again, and she would often sit in the studio with him, reading, or otherwise occupying herself, while he created his works of art. Though the young wife was a quiet woman, when she did speak, she usually said something simple, yet profound. Sometimes, the artist could not grasp what she meant; she seemed not to be of this world.

After a brief honeymoon period, the artist once again prepared to open his doors to prospective buyers of his paintings. Nervously, as the first lot lined up outside, he paced back and forth in the studio, afraid that the potion was no longer working. His anxiety was mounting by the minute, until finally, he could stand it no longer. He had to know.

He stopped in his tracks, staring at the door, bracing himself for the worst possible outcome. Drawing in a very deep breath, he marched toward the door, as if somehow, his appearance of courage might alter the situation.

In they filed, one at a time, having heard of this very great artist and his magnificent work. The man scarcely took a breath as he watched them moving amongst his paintings, biting his lip as he waited to hear the response.

At last, he heard it. The familiar 'ooohs' and 'aaaahs', to which he had become accustomed, and his customers began to make their selections, still paying unbelievably horrendous prices for his work.

'Ah,' he thought, 'All is right in my world.' But then, another thought struck him, and it felt like a bucket of cold water, emptied directly on his head. He was always in such a rush to put the potion on the paintings, so that he could hang and sell them, it had been quite some time since he had bothered to check to see how much of it remained. He had always known the bottle would someday be emptied, but he had chosen not to give it much thought; it had been too distressing to consider.

As the sun poured through the castle window, the artist slipped away from his customers for a few moments into a little room off the studio, and fetched the bottle of Transformation Potion from its secret hiding place in the stone wall. He was stunned to notice that the bottle was almost empty! He had not realized that it was disappearing, though when he thought about it, he had been using it for a very long time, and frankly, it was amazing that it has lasted all those years. He felt a sudden resurgence of his boyhood fears, welling up in his stomach and rising to his throat. This alarmed the man, as he knew that when it was gone, he would no longer be raking in the money as he had been doing.

'Well,' he thought to himself, 'I have no choice but to charge even more exorbitant prices for my work while I still have some of this potion.' And this is exactly what he did.

The miserly artist soon seemed to forget how smitten he had been with his lovely wife, and he spent more and more time with his painting, returning to his old habit of creating day and night. Rapidly, she grew bored, watching him at the easel every waking minute. Many times, she tried to speak with him, and she usually got a distracted grunt or 'hm' in response. Eventually, he did not even seem to notice when she entered the room.

Late one winter's night, as the artist stood at his easel, painting again by the light of one small candle, still conserving his vast amounts of money, he was suddenly struck by the feeling that he was not alone, that he was being watched. Instantly, he recalled the night the old crone appeared in his little cottage. As the hair on the back of his neck stood on end once again, he was quite certain that this was the moment he had once dreaded, but had long since put out of his head.

Slowly turning around, there, in the shadows, was a cloaked figure, silent and unmoving.

This time, the artist was not so afraid, yet he was nervous about what might be asked of him. "Come out of the shadows, Old Woman! Show yourself!" he commanded.

After a moment or two, the crone stepped into the dim and flickering light of the candle. The two faced each other, recalling their first meeting.

Finally, the old hag spoke. "I have come with my request. As you well know, I honoured my promise, and now it is your turn to honour yours. Are you ready to do as I ask?"

Nervously, the man swallowed and replied, "Yes. Hurry up with it, then. You are wasting my time."

His curt reply seemed to annoy the old woman, as a look of disdain crossed her twisted face.

"There is a little boy who needs your help. His parents are dead and he has no means of supporting himself. He is a very gifted artist, but cannot afford food, much less paints and canvas. You will give him some money, keeping him fed, sheltered, and painting."

The artist was stunned. What a terrible thing to ask! He could not fathom parting with his money, especially not when he was just about out of transformation potion. He had to keep every bit of money he had. And to expect him to give any of it to someone whom he saw as his rival? Preposterous! He was not about to see some starving little orphan grow up to take his place in the art world, and he certainly was not going to be the one responsible for his own fall from the pedestal upon which he had been placed. It was true, he believed he deserved to be there. But in reality, it was magic that had created the situation, yet he did not wish to acknowledge this.

He took a few moments to consider the old woman's request, and then flatly refused to comply. Her dark eyes flashed in anger, her thin lips were pressed together in a stern line.

"You have almost run out of the Transformation Potion. Does this not concern you?" she asked, knowingly.

"Of course not!" he lied, growing more nervous. "And just how would you know how much I have left? For all you know, I may have run out long ago!"

"I know many things," she replied, mysteriously. "And even without my special abilities, I know that no one would buy any of your work, unless you had applied the potion. You are still selling your dreadful paintings, and at unreasonable prices. But you will not sell one more when the potion runs out."

The artist's anxiety ripped through his stomach and flew directly to his heart, clutching at it with desperation. But of course, he did not want the old crone to see this. As calmly as he could manage, he looked directly into her squinted and ugly little eyes. "You will see that you are wrong. I now have an excellent reputation. Everyone knows that I am the greatest artist who ever lived, and they will still want to buy my paintings, just to say they own my work, even if they do not like it. That is what people do, so my future is quite safe. I no longer need your potion."

The old woman's eyes flashed again. Giving him a moment to allow his feelings of discomfort to grow, she rather enjoyed watching him attempt to hide it.

"And what is your answer, then, about the boy?" she queried.

"I have given you my answer. Ask me for something else, but I refuse to part with my money, and I most certainly will not promote a child who could oust me from my current position. He will have to find his own way; his problems are none of my concern."

The crone stood in silence for a few moments, and then asked, "Are you quite certain that this is your answer? You do not wish to reconsider?"

"Yes, that is my answer, and I will not reconsider," he replied, emphatically. "You are asking far too much of me."

The old hag contemplated reminding him of what she had done for him, but well knew the comment would be lost on him entirely. Rather, she simply stated, "I always keep my promises."

And with that, she vanished before his eyes.

The artist stood in silence for a moment, wondering whether there might be some consequence for his refusal of her request. He had not thought to ask her this; it had not occurred to him as she stood before him. His only thoughts at that time had been for his money. Nervously, he turned back to his painting, unsuccessfully trying to shake off the nagging feeling that he had not yet seen the last of the crone.

Once again, the man had a very restless night after his visit from the old woman. He tossed and turned, thrashed and fretted until the wee hours, when he finally dozed off, exhausted from worry.

A couple of hours later, the man awoke, and with still-closed eyes, was aware of sunlight pouring into the room. It took a few moments before the events of the previous night flooded back into his memory, and with them, came the anxiety. Finally opening his eyes and focusing on the room around him, he sat bolt upright in bed, horrified! 'No!' he thought, 'This must be another nightmare!' Shutting his eyes hard and shaking his head, he tried to convince himself that what he saw could not possibly be real.

Opening his eyes once more, he saw that he was sitting in bed in his run-down little cottage. Everything was exactly as it had been on that night so long before, that night the old crone had come to call. He was horrified! What was happening? How could this be? Where was his wife? A million questions ripped through his mind like daggers, as he tried to understand.

He crept out of bed and wandered through the tiny cottage, seeing everything exactly as he remembered it being on the night that the old crone had come to him. There were a few bits of bread in the cupboard, several nearly-empty tubes of paint, his worn, old brushes, the one small piece of candle, and of course, a few pennies in the jar. The only difference was that the paintings were all gone.

After a few moments' silence, as the artist struggled to absorb the shock of this very rude awakening, he suddenly let out a horrific, long scream, before collapsing on the floor in tears.

The days passed. The man's hair had turned completely white from shock, and he had fallen into a state of very ill health from fear and a lack of food. He wished that he had some supplies so that he could begin painting again, believing that he could earn some money. "After all," he said out loud, "People used to love... my..." His voice trailed off, suddenly hit with the knowledge that the crone had been right; they had only loved his paintings because of the Transformation Potion.

And in that moment, as much as he thought his whole world has already fallen apart, it came crashing down around his ears with the knowledge that he was not, after all, an artist. He never was, and never would be. All his childhood fears of starvation and poverty had now become a living nightmare. His attempts to relieve his greatest fears had only brought him more of the same. It was too much to bear! A lifetime of dreams and ambitions, shattered and lying in pieces around him in the blink of an eye.

If he thought he was broken entirely on the morning when he found himself in his cottage again, he had been as mistaken as a man could be. Every part of him was crushed, smashed, absolutely blown to pieces. He had only ever had one dream, and that was to become a magnificent artist. Never had he considered any other career. He was trained in nothing, and had only ever done odd jobs to earn money. He had no idea what his future held. It was as barren, black and empty as it could possibly be. At that moment, he desperately wished that he would just die. He believed that he could not be so lucky, however; he was certain that he had no right to die and escape his misery. He had been such a fool, such a hateful and selfish fool. And now he must reap the rewards of such a lifetime.

Being the middle of winter, it was dreadfully cold and biting outside. With no fuel for the fire, it was not much better in his cottage, but at least he was protected from the wind and the snow.

He had never known hunger like this. His belly ached from morning till night, and he felt increasingly weak and ill. One night, he felt he could stand it no longer. He desperately needed food, and maybe a few logs for his fire. Wrapping himself in an old, thin coat, his only protection from the harsh night air, he stumbled outside and down the road.

Knocking on doors, he begged for help. Several concerned faces appeared as doors were opened to him, but the concern quickly became disgust, anger or resentment when the villagers realized who it was who needed their assistance. The doors would soon be closed, sometimes with a few unkind words, other times with complete silence.

It was not long before he began to have increasingly vivid recollections of all the times someone had knocked on his door, offering friendship or asking for help. And for the first time in his life, he began to experience remorse and compassion. As he walked, stooped over, head down against the wind, hoping to find just one kind soul who would be willing to help him, he was overcome with shame and he began to weep. The tears froze on his icy cheeks, but he did not notice; he was consumed by his guilt and realized that he had, indeed, got exactly what he deserved, just as the crone had promised.

Stumbling along through the wind and snow, the artist reviewed his life and his choices. He saw that he had been exceedingly selfish and greedy, that he had never cared about another living soul, except for his young wife. Sadly, he realized that even with her, with his beautiful bride, he had taken her for granted, and had once again allowed his selfishness to rule his life.

He thought about how he had used magic to sell his paintings, and even worse, that he had been paid ridiculous sums of money which often caused serious financial hardship for people, ruining many lives and creating the same kind of situation for them as he had detested enduring as a child. His own experience with hunger and fear for his survival and future were only the tiniest glimpse into what he had done to countless people through the years. And all the while, he had cared only about himself and his money. One after another, his sins and his failings came to him, slamming into his head and his heart, creating such torment that he could bear it no longer.

At that moment, he collapsed in the snow, sobbing loudly but uncaring, as he finally understood just who he had been all those years.

Not far from where he lay, frozen and starving in the snow, there was a tiny little cottage. The flickering firelight in the window was warm and inviting. But the artist did not see it.

Inside the cottage, a woman and her three young sons were preparing to have their sparse evening meal. Their clothes were in tatters, and they were all very thin. One of the children suddenly cried, "Did you hear that?!" Everyone was silent. They could hear only the howling and whistling of the wind.

But then, there was something else. "There!" he cried, "There it is again!" They listened a little harder, the mother going to the window and peering outside.

The little boy said, "It sounds like someone crying, Mother!"

And as she looked outside, the mother thought she saw a crumpled figure, lying in the snow.

"Quickly!" she said to the two older boys. "Get your coats and get him inside!"

The boys did as they were told, and in a couple of minutes, they had managed to help the man stumble into the warmth of their cottage, his head hanging, not entirely aware of what was happening around him.

They sat him in a chair by the fire, and it was then that the woman saw who he was. He did not see the look on her face, and it was just as well, given his current condition, and all that he had just come to understand.

The woman said not a word, but promptly drew some steaming water from a kettle in the fireplace, and made a cup of tea for the man. She covered him with two thin blankets, tucking them in around him, and lifted his feet onto the hearth. By the time he had sipped at his tea, and had been warmed by the fire, he was able to compose himself a little. Looking up at the woman standing beside him, his eyes filled with tears. Choking on the lump in his throat, he humbly thanked her.

She made no reply, nor did she smile at him, but rather, she turned and gathered the children around the table. Retrieving a pot of very thin soup from the fireplace, she set it on the table, and set out a small amount of bread on a plate next to it. After ladeling out a portion of the soup for each child, she put the last of it into a bowl, took a small piece of the bread, and offered these to the man. Incredulous, he stared at her, at her offering, and at the table, realizing that there was no more food for herself.

"No, please, you are very kind, but that is the last of your food. I cannot accept it."

She stood silently over him, still offering the bowl and the bread. Once again he politely refused, feeling even more guilt and shame than he had while he lay out in the snow.

Placing the bowl and the bread on a tiny table next to his chair, she said, "Please. Eat. It is not much, but it is all I have to offer, and you need it far more than I."

He looked at the tattered clothing on the family's thin bodies, and realized the enormity of this gift. He knew he was entirely undeserving, but the woman seemed insistent.

At last, too weak from hunger, from cold, and from emotion, he began to eat the soup. There was not much in it, but it was the best meal he had ever eaten. Just before he had come inside this beautiful little cottage, he was certain he was moments away from Death, which would have been a blessed relief at that time. And now, with each spoonful of soup, he felt Life returning, coursing through his veins, both body and soul being nourished by the woman's most generous gift.

After he had finished the meager meal, the woman noticed that he had a little colour in his face. He looked very drawn and haggard, and his hair was entirely white, but there was no mistaking who he was. She mustered her courage and asked him, "Do you know who I am?"

He studied her face, believing that her query meant he should be able to answer, 'Yes.' However, he could not. Immediately, he felt shame. So many faces in the village, so many people lived right near him for much of his life, yet he knew no one.

"I'm so sorry, Ma'am, but no, I do not know you."

"I thought not," was her simple reply, and she wore an expression that he could not begin to describe. "My husband and I knocked on your door, wanting to befriend you on several occasions, but you always turned us away. Eventually, we had decided not to return, since you clearly seemed to have no interest.

"But one day, my husband and I suddenly felt compelled to go to you for one of your paintings," she continued. "It was an exorbitant amount of money, costing every bit of our savings, and more.

"It was the strangest thing. It was as though we were under a spell. We both knew that it was entirely wrong, that we had children to feed, and bills to pay, yet it was as though something was forcing us, compelling us to buy your painting, even though we knew it was a terrible idea. It was as though we had no choice, no will of our own."

She grew silent for a moment, and the man felt even more shame and guilt wash over him than before. There were no words for this inside him, only raw emotion.

"Soon after we bought the painting, it was as though we were cursed. Our tiny daughter, a very healthy and robust wee girl, suddenly became very ill and died. Immediately after that, my husband lost his job and could not find another. And then, with all the strain, he fell into such a deep depression that he took his own life."

The artist sat in stunned silence, not having any idea what he could possibly say to this woman, and feeling entirely responsible for every bit of her loss and her pain. Once again, the tears began to fall.

As she continued her story, her voice changed and became quietly angry. "After my husband died, I felt more certain than ever that the painting was cursed. I could not wait to get rid of it. In a fit of rage and grief one night, I tore it down from the wall, and smashed the frame, throwing the pieces and the canvas into the fire. I was certain that it had come from Hell, and I wanted it to go back there, far away from me and my sons."

The man could only weep in response, his face buried in his hands, as he repeated "I'm sorry! I'm so sorry!" over and over again.

The woman left him to his remorse and the room fell quiet, except for the man's sobs, which gradually subsided until he was entirely spent. The woman just sat opposite him, rocking by the fire and staring into it, her eyes indicating that she was a million miles away, lost in her grief.

A little while later, the woman refilled the man's tea, poured some for herself and the children, then returned to her chair. The two sat in silence for some time, until the woman spoke, telling her children it was time for bed. After goodnight kisses between mother and sons, the boys disappeared to their tiny bedroom.

Alone for the first time that evening, the silence suddenly

felt awkward. Realizing that it was time to leave, but struggling to find the right words to say, the man stood, clearing his throat. Wrapping his thin coat tightly around himself before heading back into the cold, he turned to face the woman.

"I have to ask you," the man said, hesitating for a moment. "After all you have been through because you bought my painting, and after how unbearably rude I had been to you in the past, why did you take me in and treat me with such kindness?"

"It is simple," she said. "We all make mistakes and we are all deserving of forgiveness. You needed my help, so I gave it to you."

The artist was overcome with emotion. Choking back more tears, he offered the woman a warm hug, knowing no other way to express what was in his heart. She accepted it, and after he thanked her profusely, she sent him on his way with a few logs under his arm, and a little packet of nuts and dried fruit in his pocket.

The man had much to consider on his way home; he felt like a new man. His life was going to be very different, as different as it could possibly be.

The cottage was, of course, in darkness upon his return, yet the bright, full moon shed enough light through the window that the man could see his way to the hearth. Quickly, he laid a fire, and as he struck a match to light the bit of paper under the logs, he was startled to see a pile of wood stacked neatly along the stone wall beside him. Bewildered, he tried to figure out who would have left him such a gift, but he could find no answer to the question.

He sat there, on the floor, staring into the fire, contemplating many things, trying to find a place to begin to put his life right and to try to repair some of the damage he had caused. It was a most daunting task, and he felt completely overwhelmed. When he had been warmed by the flames, he stood and turned to face his tiny sitting room, which was bathed in the beautiful glow from the fire. As he began to move across the room to hang up his coat and put away the woman's gifts of nuts and fruit, something caught his eye. Turning his head, he was stunned to see a basket of new brushes and tubes of paint, and a large roll of canvas, sitting on the table in a corner.

"What is this?" he wondered out loud in astonishment. "Who is leaving me these beautiful gifts, and why?"

Initially, upon seeing the painting supplies, he was thrilled and elated about being able to paint again. But his expression of joy suddenly turned to one of defeat, as his face fell, remembering that he was not an artist after all.

He sank down into a chair, wondering what should be done with these gifts, believing that he had no need of them, when suddenly, he noticed in the pit of his stomach, the tiniest seed of an old, familiar feeling. It was the desire to paint, and it felt like the return of a long-lost friend. He was made a little nervous by it, for he well remembered how it felt to have his dreams shattered before his very eyes, and he was not too eager to experience it again. But something felt different. The more he focused on the desire, the more it grew, until it seemed that it rose up from his stomach and into his heart, filling every part of his being with a burning need to create.

He had never experienced anything quite like this before, but he was unable to identify what was different. He remembered being driven to paint in the past; it was his constant companion from his earliest days, and it was only in recent days that he realized there had been no point.

40

What was this, then? This was a different kind of need, a different kind of burning desire.

Despite the darkness in the room, the artist felt compelled to stretch some canvas onto a frame and set it on his easel by the fire, where he had enough light by which he could paint. He was in a dreadful hurry to begin creating, and could not open the tubes of paint quickly enough, and spread beautiful colour onto the pallet. Grabbing his brushes, his hand flew from pallet to canvas and back again, applying broad, swift strokes as he worked.

Never had he felt anything like this before! It seemed that everything in his heart was flying straight down his arm, through the brush and onto the canvas! It was as though a dam had burst and everything inside him came rushing out in a flood.

He did not stop at one painting; he continued long into the night, until finally, the sun was coming up, lighting the room with the dawn of a new day. At last, he felt he could stop and take a breath. Standing back from the paintings which stood propped and drying around the room, in the morning light, he had his first good look at the fruits of his labour.

The artist was absolutely stunned beyond words. His eyes grew wide and his mouth fell open. He could truly say that these were, indeed, very beautiful works of art, completely unlike anything he had ever created in the past. They were full of life and emotion, passion and colour. In disbelief, he sank into a chair, exhausted, exhilarated, and weeping as he smiled, gazing at his incredible paintings.

He was not certain how long he had been asleep, but he awoke some time later, to discover that he had nodded off in his chair. In his sleepiness, before opening his eyes, he wondered if his night of painting had all been a dream, and was almost afraid to open his eyes. But open them he did. And there, still propped against walls and furniture, were his very beautiful creations.

Rising to stretch, stiff from his hours in the chair, the artist began to cross the room to have a closer look at each of his paintings. As he did so, he noticed another basket, perched on the windowsill, and this one was filled with food. There were fruits and vegetables, a large piece of cheese, and a crusty loaf of bread. Once again, he was astonished, puzzled about how and why these beautiful gifts could have possibly been given to him, and by whom. His heart filled with wonder and gratitude, as he helped himself to some of the contents, feeling very undeserving.

As the artist sat alone, enjoying his delicious meal, he gazed around the room at his creations and wondered what he would do with them. Certainly, no one would buy them after the life had previously led, but he was at peace with that knowledge, and decided he would try to give them away. It would have been wrong to attempt to sell them, after how horribly selfish and greedy he had been in the past. Of one thing, he was certain: he MUST paint. Whether or not anyone else ever saw one of his works of art again, he would continue to paint for the sake of self-expression, knowing that there was a piece of his soul in each of his creations.

Thoughts of his lovely wife rolled through his head. He loved her so much, and was so filled with regret about having lost her because of his greed. He wondered where she was, and desperately wished that she could see him now, longing to tell her of the changes in him, and to show her his new paintings. Sadly, he realized that although he would always love her, she was lost to him forever.

During the night, the winter storm had passed, making way for a warmer, brighter day. Late in the afternoon, the artist went for a very long walk down the road and through the forest. He noticed his surroundings in a way that he never had before. The smell of the pine, the crunch of the snow under his feet, the little birds who searched for berries and seeds... he was especially touched by them, and felt compassion for the starving little birds; he had become well-acquainted with how it felt to be hungry and to fear for one's own survival. He wished that he had some seeds to give them, and suddenly found himself wishing he could feed and help any living soul who was in need.

At that moment, a thought struck him, making him stop dead in his tracks. He remembered the young boy, the one the crone had asked him to help. Suddenly, he was filled with a great need to see if he could find this boy and offer him -- offer him what? He had nothing to give. He was not even certain about how he was going to be able to look after himself, much less a boy in as much need as that child was. His heart sank, momentarily having been so excited about having an opportunity to make a difference in the child's life, only to realize that he could do nothing.

Hanging his head as he continued to walk in the fading light of the setting sun, he felt so ashamed and remorseful. He could have done so much for the boy when he had all the riches of several kingdoms, had he not been so greedy and jealous. Thoroughly disgusted with himself for having left an innocent child to suffer, he could barely stand to think about it. Not only did that child deserve to have a home and food, but he deserved the chance to become the artist that the crone had told him the boy was destined to be.

He recalled his own youth, the poverty in which he had lived, and his dreams of escaping it and being a great artist.

He well remembered the fear and the pain that his impoverished existence had caused him in his childhood, and he could not stand to think that he had lost an opportunity to remove the same kind of fear and pain for another boy. And worse, that boy's parents had died; he could not believe that he had turned his back on the child. Filled with shame and regret, and wondering what would become of the boy, he wearily made his way back home.

It was dark when he arrived back at his little cottage. The air outside has grown colder as the sun sank into the night. Stepping inside, he stamped the snow off his boots, and found his way to the hearth. Kneeling there in the dark, preparing a fire, he felt that familiar prickling up the back of his neck as the hairs stood on end.

'Oh, no!' he thought. 'How much worse can it get? What else can she do to me?!' He felt totally beaten and defeated, and unprepared to do battle with the old crone. Though he had learned many valuable lessons, he did not believe that it would matter to her at all. She would exact her revenge; of that, he was certain.

He worked quickly and quietly, until he had finished lighting the fire. He was grateful for its warmth, as he sat, rubbing his hands together in front of it, all the while, knowing the crone was standing directly behind him. Without turning around, he finally said, with some exasperation, "What is it you want from me now? You've taken everything I had, and I learned many lessons. I have nothing else to give you, there is nothing else you can take away. What can you possibly want?"

There was a brief silence, followed by the now familiar sound of the rustling cloak.

"You," was the brief reply.

The artist was puzzled. What could she mean by that? Was she going to kill him? But the voice -- the voice was not right. It sounded like... No!

He spun around in shock and disbelief, for there stood his beautiful wife in a long, black cloak. Her hair, so dark and long, hung softly framing her delicate face and smooth, white skin.

"What -- what --" was all that came out of his mouth, as he stood to face her. His wife smiled and delighted in his confusion and the surprise.

"How did you find me?" he asked, obviously not comprehending what was happening.

"I always know where you are. I have found you before."

"What do you mean? It was I who found you when we met. How do you always know where I am? I do not understand," he said, a look of bewilderment on his face.

"I mean, here, years ago, that night, and not long ago, at the castle..." She waited for him to figure it out. But he did not.

"The Transformation Potion, darling," she said, in a matter-of-fact way.

His eyes grew wide and he was at once astonished and horrified. "You!" he cried. "You are the crone?"

His lovely young wife smiled again, nodding as he finally understood.

"No! It cannot be! How..." The man was both speechless and horrified.

Again, she simply said, "The Transformation Potion, darling." And as she watched her husband recoil, she began to laugh.

The artist was faint from the shock, from the surprise, and had to sit, while his wife began to explain. "I was sent to teach you many lessons. Do you remember the promise that I made to you?"

"Yes," replied the artist, "of course I do. You promised to give me all I deserved, and you did, every step of the way. Though the lessons have been harsh, I needed them."

"You are right," said his beautiful young bride, "you did, and you have learned them well. You have learned that what is important in life is not what we can get, but what we can give. You have learned to have compassion, respect and responsibility. You have learned that you cannot run from yours fears; they will follow you everywhere, and will destroy you, if you so allow it. You have understood that even if you had created a beautiful painting, you forgot who your customers would be, and you treated everyone with rudeness, disrespect and arrogance. But through your suffering, you have mastered many lessons, not the least of which is something else right here in this room."

The artist was further confused. To what could she be referring? He looked around the room, searching for a clue to his wife's puzzle.

"The answer lies in your paintings, my love," she continued. "Just look around you, and see what you have created."

The artist's eyes scanned the room, as they went from painting to painting. Each one seemed to reach back out to him and speak to him, an echo of something deep in his soul. He thought he was beginning to understand.

"As a child, you lived in poverty. You were consumed by it, terrified by it, and could not see all the riches of having two parents who loved and supported you and your dreams, and who did their best for you. For years, your paintings were created out of your fear and your desire for money, which you thought would bring you happiness and peace.

"You had everything you needed, but all you saw was what you wanted and did not have, and your paintings told only the story of fear, and of greed and selfishness. They did not speak of love, or respect, gratitude or passion for anything except money. It was impossible for you to create anything desirable, as long as that was all that lived in your heart.

"But look around you, my love. These paintings speak volumes about all that is of value. There is compassion in these creations, there is humility, there is a soul, living and breathing in every one of them. You are no longer concerned with making a fortune with your gift; you only wish to paint purely for the love of it, for the love of expressing what is in your heart. Now you understand what it is to be a truly great artist."

The man stood in silence, absorbing all that his wife had told him. Finally, he realized what it was that had been different the night before, as he had been creating all these paintings. All the pieces of the puzzle were falling into place, and it was beginning to make sense to him.

With so much to overwhelm the artist, it had taken this long, but all of a sudden, another question rushed into his mind. "What about the crone? And you? I do not understand! How can you be one and the same? Why did you come to me as that horrible old woman?"

Smiling, his wife replied, "As I told you, I was sent to teach you many lessons. My appearance has always reflected what was in your heart. I came to you in your dreams, and then here and at the castle, reflecting the ugliness of what you held inside."

The artist felt somewhat embarrassed and ashamed by her statements, but he could not deny their truth.

"Do you remember the day we met?" she asked.

"Oh, but of course!" he replied.

"Think back," she said, "and remember what was happening immediately before you saw me on the cliffs."

The man closed his eyes, recalling that day as he stood on the balcony, delighting in the beauty of the ocean, the sun, feeling a sense of appreciation and peace that he had not known before. It was then that he had spotted her on the beach.

He did not need to say a word as he recalled these thoughts and feelings, because his wife spoke again. "Yes, you do remember. That little bit of appreciation for what was around you, for the gifts of the Universe, that was what prompted me to appear to you in the form in which you saw me on that day. And when you had returned to ugliness, I came to you once more as the crone."

He needed no further explanation, and he had to agree with her entirely. Everything inside him had been unbearably ugly, except for a little while after he had met and married her. He recalled his slide from that lovely place, and was horrified when her comment about her last visit as the crone jogged his memory about the child that he had abandoned.

"The boy!" he cried suddenly, "What about the boy that you wanted me to help? What will become of him? What can I do to help him? I no longer have anything to offer, but I so wish that I could turn back the clock and help him on his way!"

"I know you do, my darling, but it has already been done. You have already done everything he needed."

Once again, the artist was confused. "But I have done nothing! Nothing but abandon the lad!" he said, shame and guilt washing over him as before.

His wife laughed, tossing her head back, the hood falling to her back. "You were the boy, my love."

The artist was not used to spending so much time in a state of confusion, and was beginning to grow frustrated with the continual adding of pieces to the puzzle. Every time he thought he had it figured out, his wife threw something else in his path. "What could you possibly mean?" he asked of her. "You said this was a boy whose parents had died, and he was destined to be a wonderful and gifted artist. My parents died when I was grown, and I have never been any kind of artist, only a man who painted in order to become rich!" he exclaimed.

"But you are wrong, my love. 'Tis true, you were, in a way, grown when your parents died. But you have always been that fearful little boy, living in poverty, and screaming to get out of it. Even as an adult, you were still that hungry child who was destined to become a great artist. You had grown used to your monetary wealth, and had forgotten where you had begun. And when I came to you that night to make my request, your fear drove you to commit one of the worse possible crimes against the soul. You turned your back on yourself."

She let her words sink in, and saw her husband hang his head in shame, understanding more than he wanted to. After a moment, he looked up at her and asked, "With all of the terrible things I have done, how am I destined to become a great artist?"

Waving her hand around the room, she gestured toward the paintings, she waited for his eyes to follow. Her husband's brow still carried the furrows of a puzzled man.

"I still do not understand," he said quietly, looking from his paintings back to his wife. "A great artist? But how? I have turned so many away from me, and cannot imagine that anyone would ever buy a painting from me again, no matter how beautiful it might be."

Once again, the artist's wife laughed, and she replied, "First of all, you will find that there is much forgiveness in the world. There are many who will give you another chance when they see all that you have learned. And secondly, much of the damage that was caused by your selfishness will be undone, reversed."

The man thought back to the kind young widow, whose husband and daughter were dead because of his actions. Surely, that could not be undone. He began to speak, but as in the past, his wife seemed to reading his mind. "Yes, you are right," she said, "Death cannot be reversed. But all the people who have suffered financial hardship and loss will find that the damage will be repaired before long."

And unbeknownst to the artist, as she spoke these words, the widow was about to find baskets of food and new clothing in her cottage, the first of many such gifts which would help her along the way. And at the same moment, in countless other homes across the land, similar gifts were appearing, as there had been great magic and healing power in the artist's awakening.

The man sank into a chair by the fire, overwhelmed by all that he had been told that evening. His wife followed, and sat in the one next to him.

Looking into her eyes, his own filled with tears. "I am so relieved to know the truth about the boy. I did not know how I was going to live with myself, knowing that I had turned my back on a child I had been able to help, a child who needed my love and the stability of a safe home."

His wife smiled, and leaning forward, took his hands in hers. "You will have another chance, my love. There is another child who needs you."

The artist's eyebrows shot up, and he sat straight in his chair, eager for a chance to redeem himself. "Who? Who is it? What can I do? I have nothing, really, to offer, but please, tell me what to do! I will move heaven and earth to make a difference for this child!"

"I know you will," she replied, and taking one of his hands, she placed it on her belly, which he noticed was a little larger than when he had last seen his wife. It took a moment for him to understand what was happening, and then he felt a tiny movement under his hand, which startled him, causing him to pull his hand away, and stare in surprise at his wife.

"Yes, my love," she said, smiling warmly at him. "We have created a child who needs his father, and you will be able to teach him all the things you have learned. You will, indeed, be a great artist, but it will be because you have a great understanding of what is really valuable in life. These are things you will pass on to our son, and to the other children who will follow."

The artist could not believe his ears! This had been the most magical evening of his life, the right kind of magic. He threw his arms around his wife, and kissed her passionately, as tears began to stream down his face. His heart overflowed with many emotions for which he could find no words. They welled up into his throat, causing a lump bigger than he had ever felt before. All he could do was hold his beautiful wife in love, respect, and deep gratitude.

After a long embrace, the man pulled himself away. Blinking at his wife through his tears, he smiled the warmest smile he had ever felt on his face. But suddenly, a worrisome thought rolled through his mind.

"There is something troubling me," he said, an anxious tone in his voice. "You promised that I would get what I deserved. It is not right that things should turn out so beautifully for me. I have earned the position in which I have found myself," referring, of course, to his return to poverty, and seeing the scornful expressions on the faces of everyone who knew him.

Once again, his wife took his hands in hers, and looked deep into his eyes. "You are exactly right, my darling, you have earned the position in which you have found yourself. And that is the position of being a wonderful man, who has suffered and learned much, who has the love of an adoring wife, who will become a loving father, and who is already a great artist.

"Your lessons, your learning and your soul are now

powerfully reflected in your paintings, and they are meant to help others in their own healing," she continued. "Soon, you will have the fame and fortune that you have always desired, but you no longer want them for yourself. You will use them to teach, to help and to heal others, and this will mean more to you than money ever did. You will get exactly what you deserve.

"I told you, I always keep my promises."

And they lived happily ever after.

Ghostly Echoes

One of the most important things that I've learned in my personal spiritual journey is that perspective is everything. How we choose to look at a particular memory or event can dramatically alter how we feel about it.

One of my favourite minor examples of how our perspective can change how we feel is when I listen to people moaning about the weather in England (which they often do, and admit to it quite readily!). With its gentle, moderate climate, I am quick to tell them about the extremes of Calgary's weather; they are horrified to imagine temperatures in the minus 40s. Suddenly, England doesn't seem so cold.

Sometimes our memories of an event are improved with a different perspective; other times not.

This short piece was written, with a bit of 'artistic licence', about something which was, at one time in my life, extremely important and soul-saving. It speaks about my perspective years earlier when I was a child, and compares it with my perspective as an adult.

Ghostly Echoes

I suppose whether or not something is different from the way it used to be is really much more complicated than one might first realize. My feelings tell me that The Farm, which had always been everything to me, has now become totally different, completely changed. But has it really? I used to live for my summer trips to The Farm, for my visits with my grandparents, aunt, uncle and cousins who lived there. Now I have no desire to return at all because in my heart, it is not the place I remember loving so much as a child. I cannot bear to see it.

I remember so vividly the land around The Farm and the intense feelings I had about it. As we drew nearer, I would become so excited it always felt as though the car was barely moving, like when you're trying to run in a dream and you feel like your legs are in quicksand, and it was all I could do not to get out and push the stupid car.

At the top of the last hill was the old one-room schoolhouse and lots of trees and shrubbery hiding the intersecting roads; hence, the long-practiced custom of honking just before you got there. Just a short distance away, there was one last curve -- oh, how I used to love that curve -- with its thick, lush, green trees and bushes lining the old dirt road, deep with familiar, somehow comforting ruts. Finally, after we rounded the curve, there it was. The most delightful, wonderful, magical place on the face of the earth -- The Farm -- complete with a big, red barn, nestled into the trees around the curve, livestock, crabapple trees, fresh berries, the lake not too far off, endless hours of laughter and exciting things to do, and most important of all, The House.

I wonder how much of my life has been spent in that house, although most of it was while I was 600 miles away. It was such a cozy old house, with its lovely creaking floors; soft, lumpy furniture, the Big Stool in the kitchen, which was SO tall and very difficult to climb; the pitcher and basin on the rough, wooden washstand in my room; the robin's-egg-blue walls throughout the entire house, and doilies on everything; the old black wood stove; the familiar, rhythmic creaking and groaning of the green water pump in the utility room; the pail full of fresh, icy well water with a dipper in it, in case we were thirsty, and chamber pots for later; the ancient iron bed that swallowed me in its softness, feather pillows and quilts, sewn by my grandmother with love; heavenly smells of bread or cinnamon buns baking, chicken and dumplings, fresh, warm applesauce, and a myriad of other delights always filled the house -- I can still remember. And I can still see Grandma standing in the kitchen, usually cooking. No one ever really loved me except Grandma. The House always warmed me when nothing else could ease the chill of my loneliness; even when I was far away, The Farm worked its magic. For years, the pain in my life was soothed only by the comforting memories, or anticipation of time spent on The Farm.

But now the roads are gravel; the ruts are gone. The desire to travel on them is gone. The trees and shrubs on the hill are gone; no one honks any more. A straight, bare, dry road now pushes its way through the place where the curve used to be. The barn is gone; burned to the ground. My grandmother and grandfather are gone. The meaning -- the all-important, soul-saving meaning is gone.

The House, however, is still there. The floors would creak more lovingly now, but no one walks on them any more, except the mice who scamper across them, in a hurry to hide from -- no one. The pitcher and basin are still there, but no one uses them any more. The furniture is softer and lumpier, but no one sits on it any more. The Big Stool isn't very big any more; in fact, it's small enough to be uncomfortable now. The heavenly warm kitchen smells have been replaced by dust, stale air, pungent mothballs (protecting what?). Grandma's sunny bedroom, which always smelled of her perfume, is gone, ripped apart after she died, and it was turned into a bathroom, now full of rusted fixtures from the lousy water.

If you stood ever so quietly and listened ever so carefully, you might still hear the lovely, soothing, rhythmic creaking and groaning of that old green water pump, as it filled buckets with water to be heated and dumped into a washtub for a child's late night bath in a darkened kitchen, lit only by the flickering fire in the stove. If you closed your eyes and listened a little harder, you could hear the years' worth of sounds. They live in the walls. You could hear plates being scraped with silverware, as families delighted in the meals prepared with love; wooden matches being struck, and then their tiny explosions; hushed voices, being careful not to wake the children (-- which generation? I can't make out the voices -- maybe the fourth?); potatoes being peeled and dropped into a pot of water; beans being snapped and making very little noise as they hit the bowl; crisp, fresh lettuce being torn; sick babies being nursed; squealing children; pages being torn off calendars, and voices remarking how quickly time is passing; crying -- who is that? There's so much pain -- can you hear it? Is it an echo of the sadness of someone who lived long ago, or is it the sobbing of a lonely ghost? Maybe it is I. When I close my eyes, I feel it.

So I don't close my eyes. I don't want to feel it. I don't want to remember. Besides, it's really not so different from the past. It's pretty much the same as before, isn't it? After all, it's just an empty farm, at the end of a gravel road, and just a rickety, old white house, always was, still is, but now occupied by birds and mice. It's just four sagging, old walls...walls that tell stories if you stand in the middle of them, close your eyes, and listen.

The Story of Trust

Living with any kind of abuse is, of course, extremely difficult. And unless you have lived with it, you will not understand that it can be even more difficult to leave such a relationship. People on the outside think, "How can you stay? Just pack up and go." If it were that easy, everyone would do it in a heartbeat.

To fall into an abusive relationship, be it physical, emotional and/or sexual abuse, is a very complicated dance between people who fit together in a particularly unhealthy pattern. There is a lengthy list of factors which contribute to the creation of such a relationship, and in the continuance of it. The relationship between love and trust is very important, as one part of it. When we love someone, we often blindly trust. And we are often willing to move our boundaries and let down our guard for someone we love, trusting more, and becoming very vulnerable to attack.

The Story of Trust outlines the choreography of this dance, emphasizing how the steps and participants fit together to create it.

The Story of Trust

Once upon a time, far, far away, in the Forest of Innocence, there lived a little girl named Trust. She was very small and delicate, and she lived with her Guardian, Love, in the Castle of Self-Esteem.

Trust was a very special girl, and when she was born, the Keeper of the Castle Gate created protectors for her. These soldiers were called Boundaries, and they were led by the strongest of them all, the Boundary of Self-Respect. Whenever Trust left the safety of the Castle, they followed her while she played in the Forest.

Being the Guardian of Trust, Love had an enormous responsibility, but she was joyful and honoured upon receiving the news that she had been given this duty. Each morning, she walked through the tall, forest trees, along a well-worn path to the clear, bubbling brook and carried its precious Waters of Self-Love back to the Castle to quench Trust's thirst. Then Love would go into the Garden and pick a basketful of fresh Affirmations, upon which Trust would nibble throughout the day. Together, their lives were filled with peace and happiness.

One day, when the two of them were walking through the Forest, Love explained to Trust that when she was old enough, she would be given the Powers of the Magic of Life that would allow her to achieve anything her heart desired. As well, she would become Queen of the Forest of Innocence, and she would rule with a loving King at her side.

"For now," explained Love, "you have been given the power and responsibility to care for all the animals in the

Forest. They are vulnerable and easily wounded or killed by forces Outside the Forest. But you have the power to keep them strong and safe. All you need to do is feed them from your hand every day and they will be well."

So from that day on, when Trust went to play in the Forest, she would gather nuts, leaves and berries, calling her animal friends to her as she made her way through the trees. Trust had always loved to play with the rabbits, squirrels, deer and other Forest creatures, and she was thrilled to learn that she was responsible for keeping them well and safe from harm. She loved her task, and happily filled her skirts with the foods that sustained her beloved friends. Yes, life in the Forest of Innocence was perfect.

There was, unbeknownst to Trust, a land Outside and not so far away. It was an evil land, ruled by a horrible man. He was King Violence and his Kingdom was the Land of Abuse. His home was the Castle of Self-Loathing, and it was guarded by his soldiers, the Controllers. They were vicious, angry beasts, who protected King Violence at all costs. They fed him Power constantly, for without it, King Violence would die. They brought him water from the swirling, black, boiling River of Hate. Over the centuries, it had pulled thousands of its victims into its angry depths, sucking the very life out of their lungs and replacing it with its vile waters. And with their torturous deaths, their Power was drained from their lifeless bodies, and into the angry waters providing strength for the evil King.

The Land of Abuse was the most terrifying place on earth, filled with poisonous snakes and lizards. There were deep Pits of Abandonment, great Fires of Rage, and dark Caves of Fear and Loneliness. In its Forests of Dead Black Trees, there roamed vicious Beasts of Destruction, which devoured anything in their paths. The sun never dared go there, and the Wind howled constantly, its moans echoing hauntingly, ceaselessly throughout the Land.

The King possessed the Magic Powers of Transformation, which allowed him to make anything appear to be something other than what it was. But this was not enough for the greedy King. He also wanted to possess the Powers of the Magic of Life, for they were far stronger than his own Power, and he envied everything they would bring. He knew they would belong to the Queen of the Forest of Innocence, so he devised a wicked plan the day he heard of the birth of Trust. Then he waited for the day when she would be old enough for him to act upon it.

As the years passed, he would often peer into his cracked mirror and let out a menacing, horrible laugh as he smiled his evil smile, thinking of his plan.

"Soon, Little One, soon," he would say to the mirror, as if he were speaking to Trust herself. "The day is almost upon us." And he would rub his rough, gnarled hands together in anticipation.

Meanwhile, in the Forest of Innocence, Trust was approaching the day of her Coronation. Though it was still quite some time away, there were many preparations to be made. Soon she would be the Queen of the Forest, and all her rightful Powers would be bestowed upon her. She had grown into a very beautiful young woman, graceful, delicate and sweet. As she grew, so, too, did the Forest. It became greener, thicker, more colourful and fragrant each day that Trust lived there. It was as if the Forest knew the great significance of the coming event and was decorating itself, preparing itself to be worthy of the New Queen's rule.

King Violence also knew the day was rapidly approaching; he could hardly contain his excitement, for the time had come to begin putting his evil plan into action. One morning, he stood in front of the mirror, preparing to use his Powers of Transformation. As he stared into the mirror, the sky grew much darker than its usual dismal grey, the thick, black clouds, rolling and boiling in the ominous skies. Jagged bolts of lightning tore through the sky, immediately followed by deafening cracks of thunder. The Wind whipped through the Land, with a fierceness in its icy blast that made even the Beasts of Destruction quiver.

Suddenly, the Transformation took place. Gone was the hideous King Violence and in his stead, there stood a tall, handsome young man, with an air of dignity and royalty, and with strong, masculine features. There stood Prince Charming, dressed in the finest silk and linen, smiling to himself in the mirror as he admired his work.

Prince Charming prepared a proper coach and horses and began his journey to the Forest of Innocence. Once there, he paused for a moment outside its gates, readying himself for the task at hand. His fingers trembled with excitement as he slowly reached for the golden rings which would pull the gates open. They creaked and groaned, as it had been some time since they had been used. As they opened wide to Prince Charming, it was as if they were a mother's arms, welcoming and embracing a long-lost son.

Prince Charming's eyes grew wide when he saw the beauty of the Forest of Innocence. Hundreds of colourful butterflies floated silently through the air. The brilliance of the sunlight through the trees was almost blinding to the Prince's eyes; they were unused to its radiance. There was an explosion of colour in the thousands of unusual flowers, which burst forth from bushes, trees, the ground. Birds chirped and fluttered in the excitement of this honoured guest's arrival. The animals timidly poked their heads into the clearing, knowing something important was happening.

Nearby, under a gnarled old oak tree, Trust had just awakened from a nap in a soft bed of leaves and moss. She felt the excitement of her dear little friends and went to investigate. The energy in the Forest was dramatically different; it was almost vibrating and made Trust feel somewhat giddy. Her Boundaries felt it, too, and unsure of what it meant, they followed her closely.

Upon her arrival at the Forest entrance, Trust was met by a dashing young prince, who had eyes that looked deep into her soul, and a flashing smile that made her heart jump and beat faster than it ever had before. She felt light-headed, and had to sit on the root of a large tree to catch her breath.

Prince Charming was stunned by the beauty of Trust; never had he seen anything like it. He could not wait to possess her. He knew the only way that would happen was to first gain the confidence of Love, and then he would destroy Trust's Boundaries. "And finally," he thought to himself, "the girl will be mine."

Almost immediately after the Prince entered the Forest, Love felt his presence. She hurried to the Gate, anxious to meet the long-awaited visitor. With one look into his beautiful, dark eyes, Love new Trust's Prince had come. The Boundaries noticed that both women felt quite comfortable with this man, even though he had just barely arrived. Because of this, they relaxed their guard somewhat, and allowed him to venture nearer to Trust.

To ensure his true identity would not be discovered, with a small and unnoticed gesture of his hand, Prince Charming caused a fine mist to slowly begin to fill the Forest, so slowly that Love and Trust did not notice it was happening. But before too long, it was difficult for them to see anything clearly any more.

The Prince, Love, and Trust spent many hours together, talking, planning, sharing. The Boundaries were always close at hand, but as Trust felt increasingly safe with him, so did they, and they agreed to venture further away from their charge, at her insistence. The Prince and Trust spent endless days holding hands, walking through the Forest, and Trust allowed the Boundaries to wander further and further away with the passage of time. Gently, the Prince would stroke Trust's hair or face with his fingers. Sometimes, she would carefully take his hands in hers, and kiss them ever so sweetly, expressing her deep love for him. She adored him, adored his loving hands, which caressed her so tenderly.

As Coronation Day drew nearer, Prince Charming knew it was time to move to the next phase of his plan to further ensure his secret would remain his own. He caused a rain to fall, and once again, using his Powers of Transformation, turned the raindrops into Lie-drops, so that the Brook of Self-Love was soon filled with lies, which Love unknowingly then gave Trust to drink every day. As well, he transformed the Affirmations into Manipulation and Blame, but in the mist brought by the Prince, neither Love nor Trust noticed the difference. So when Love picked them from the bountiful garden and fed them to Trust, she was unwittingly doing the evil work of King Violence, participating in the destruction of Trust, and ultimately, in the destruction of the Forest of Innocence. His deception caused Love to destroy everything she'd worked so hard to nurture and build.

Each time the rain fell, it was harder than the last. The Lie-drops grew bigger, sometimes even so big as to cause damage to the flower petals, or the leaves of the Forest. Eventually, they had become so large as to injure the vulnerable little forest creatures. And finally, even Trust's delicate body was becoming increasingly covered with bruises.

Love began to hear Trust complain of feeling sick after eating the 'Affirmations', which neither of them knew had been transformed into Manipulation and Blame. The young girl steadily grew more ill each time Love fed her these destructive meals, yet neither had any idea what was happening. During most of this time, Love remained loyal to the Prince, never guessing that he had any part in the strange goings-on in the Forest. But when she began to notice bruises and marks on Trust's body, and saw how weak and sick Trust had become, she began to suspect the Prince's involvement.

Love went to Trust with her fears, wondering if she felt the same way. But Trust was reluctant to discuss Love's concerns. However, in the few words she spoke, Love detected the first note of unhappiness ever uttered by Trust. It broke her heart to hear it. She felt that she had failed Trust as Guardian. As well, she was upset that Trust seemed to know something was wrong, yet she was choosing to ignore it. About this, Love could do nothing.

Prince Charming was quick to pick up on Love's change of heart. Suddenly, he was filled with fear, and he felt very threatened. He became enraged and knew he had to act swiftly, before Love's suspicion grew or could be confirmed. He went to the garden to pick some Manipulation and fed it in large quantities to Love, Trust and the Boundaries. He followed it with a large pitcher of Lie-drops from the Brook. Then, when he had them all completely under his spell, the Boundaries fell asleep for the first time ever, leaving Trust completely open and vulnerable.

With that, he whisked her away to the Evil Land of Abuse and locked her in his Castle of Self-Loathing.

Once they were there, in that horrible, dark, terrifying

place, Prince Charming stood in front of Trust and smiled. But for the first time, she saw that it was not the warm smile of the man she loved, but rather the satisfied sneer of an evil, menacing stranger. As she stared at him, she began to experience real terror, a feeling from which she had been protected her whole life. Never had she endured anything so threatening. She was frightened, isolated, trapped and utterly desperate.

As she stared into the Prince's face, it began to change, slowly twisting and contorting itself into the hideous face of the Evil King Violence. His eyes no longer looked at her with love, only with rage and possesssion. She shrank away from him as he slowly moved toward her. She was out of her mind with terror. She had no Boundaries to protect her now, and the King's Controllers had silently stolen her Power and fed it to him on the way through the Gates. She was stripped of all her defences.

What happened in that Castle of Self-Loathing was more than Trust could bear. She was violated by the King in a series of the most unspeakable ways imaginable. His hands, which had once touched her so gently and sweetly, now caused her unbelievable pain and humiliation at every level of her being. She felt utterly broken and destroyed.

Over and over again, for a period of time that Trust was sure was all eternity, the King continued his reign of terror and violence. With each act of cruelty, a tiny part of Trust's heart would turn black, wither and die. By the time Trust was to have had her Coronation, there was but one small piece of her heart left. If that died, too, so would Trust.

While the King had Trust imprisoned, the Forest of Innocence had been completely destroyed in a raging fire, which left Love horribly disfigured. With Trust gone, the

Castle of Self-Esteem had crumbled. The Waters of Self-Love had disappeared, leaving the bed of the Brook dry and barren. Without Trust to feed them every day, the vulnerable Forest creatures had begun to die, one each day, until there was but one tiny little squirrel remaining alive, though seriously wounded by the Lie-drops. The Boundaries were lost, roaming aimlessly, trying to remember who and what they were, except for their leader, the Boundary of Self-Respect, who was trying desperately to find Trust. His strength was failing, however, and he knew his time was limited.

Though Trust had not actually seen the Forest for some time, she could feel its changes in her heart. On what was to be her Coronation Day, Trust sat alone in her room and began to cry. She could not believe her life had turned into this hideous nightmare, or that Love had not been able to protect her as she'd always expected. As she sat at her dressing table, looking out across the dark, terrifying, desolate Land of Abuse, a teardrop rolled down her cheek and fell on her chest, directly above the one, tiny, remaining living part of her heart.

Suddenly, she felt something strange and warm in her chest. It was a feeling of Power, and a different kind of Power from any she had known before. She had not known that even without the ceremony of her Coronation, she was to be endowed with the Powers of the Magic of Life on that day. So when this happened, she was somewhat afraid; she did not immediately understand what was happening. Soon, however, she recalled Love's words: "The Powers of the Magic of Life will allow you to achieve whatever your heart desires."

Realizing this, she began to notice a feeling of strength she had not ever felt before, and she began to believe she could escape from this horrible Land. She closed her eyes, and silently called upon her Boundaries, praying they would hear. It was difficult at first; she couldn't concentrate. But she was persistent, and found that the more she tried, the easier it became.

Wandering in the Forest, the Boundary of Self-Respect was suddenly and powerfully struck by a vision of where Trust was. As he focused on the vision, he found himself being pulled in what he believed was the right direction. His steps quickened with excitement and a growing feeling of Power. He knew then that they had begun to reconnect.

As he rushed to help Trust, he happened upon the wounded squirrel, lying alongside the path. He carefully picked it up, and carried it with him, happy to be able to protect at least one tiny, vulnerable creature. Away the two of them went, in search of the other Boundaries, readying themselves to rescue Trust.

One by one, the Boundaries were found in various states of strength and wellness after the turmoil and destruction in the Forest of Innocence. They had been wandering aimlessly, separately, powerless and unfocused. But once the group was assembled, they all noticed their strength began to grow and their focus quickly became clear.

Once they were together again, and feeling strong and clear-headed, it didn't take long for them to find the Evil Land of Abuse. They had quite a battle with the Controllers at the Gate. King Violence was there to do his best to destroy them. He was furious that Trust had gained her Power and that it was greater than his own. He felt more threatened than ever before and stepped up his efforts to take it from her.

It was a vicious, savage battle. The Boundaries and the Controllers ripped and tore at each other. Swords and axes met flesh and bone. For a while, it was difficult to tell who would win. Suddenly, Trust's Powers turned the tide and the Controllers began losing limbs and heads until soon, they were all dead. Then, using the Powers of the Magic of Life, with one final effort, she gave the Boundary of Self-Respect the strength he needed to plunge a sword into the King's black, withered heart. Instantly, the Howling Wind stopped. The Beasts of Destruction died. The River of Hate ceased its deathly churning and became still.

In the aftermath of the terrible battle, Trust, the Boundaries and the squirrel sat in the overwhelming silence, looking on with horror at the scene surrounding them. Everywhere they looked, there was a bloodied Beast, or a Controller savagely ripped apart. King Violence lay nearby, the sword which had pierced his heart, still in his chest, as if it were standing, a symbol of victory over the enemy.

Trust knew, as she sat in silence, absorbing the reality of the whole nightmare, that she would never again be as she was before meeting Prince Charming. She sat quietly stroking the squirrel, and once again, she began to cry. The wounded squirrel was even more vulnerable than when Trust had been given the responsibility for its care and safety, but her blindness had caused the deaths of all the Forest Creatures but this one. She remembered the day Love tried to speak of her concern regarding Prince Charming, but Trust had refused to listen. She remembered, too, how she had allowed her Boundaries, her Protectors, to wander, leaving herself open to the Prince's destruction. She felt ashamed because of the part she had played in the unfolding of it all.

To remind herself of not only Prince Charming's actions, but of her own responsibility in the events, she named the squirrel 'Betrayal'. She gently kissed the tiny, injured animal, who looked up at her with sad, brown eyes, and she held him to her breast, weeping as she begged for forgiveness. The squirrel looked knowingly into Trust's eyes, understanding all. Trust knew her actions would be forgiven, but not forgotten. Then magically, Betrayal disappeared from Trust's hands, and went to live in the black, withered part of her heart.

As soon as they all felt strong enough, Trust and her Boundaries began their journey back to the Forest of Innocence. When they arrived, Trust saw, for the first time, the destruction there. She fell to the ground, and wept bitterly, and was once again filled with great pain. The Forest of Innocence was no more. It was but a vast wasteland of smoldering ash, everything burned, black, dry, and dead. It was quite unrecognizable. It would be lost forever.

While absorbed in her memories, Trust was startled by a noise behind her. She turned, and gasped, horrified once again. There stood her once-beautiful Guardian, Love, her face and body dreadfully blistered, red and infected. She desperately wanted to pull Love close to her heart and hold her, but she was afraid it would cause her more pain. Love, too, wanted to embrace Trust, but her arms were so seriously injured, she did not think she could do it without spreading her infection to Trust.

The Boundaries looked on at this tragic, painful reunion. Everyone knew there was much healing to be done. And so, they all set out together, slowly walking hand in hand, journeying to the Land of Survivors.

When they arrived, they were welcomed at the Gate by several strong Boundaries. As they entered, they were most surprised to see that everyone there was terribly scarred, some more severely than others. But they all looked at Trust with the same knowing eyes with which

71

Betrayal had gazed at her. She was stunned and relieved to learn that she and her dear friends were not alone in their pain, and that healing would happen here.

Soon they were all settled into comfortable rooms in the Castle of Self-Worth. With the Boundaries of so many wise victims to guard its Gates, and with the shared strength of their new friends, they knew that together, they would learn to live with their scars.

With the Forest of Innocence totally destroyed, Trust could never again delight in its beauty. She would lie awake at night and try to recall it in detail, but her memories were lost to her pain. It was only because of the Powers of the Magic of Life that she could get through each day, knowing that they were helping her heart grow and heal. In it, there would always be Betrayal, but Trust knew that somehow, she would learn to carry on.

Grief

After my father died in January, 2004, I was driving along Deerfoot Trail in Calgary one slightly misty evening, feeling very burdened with grief and loss. Suddenly, I found myself in the thick of a very dense fog, and instantly, I felt panic because I could not see anything ahead of me. Although I knew that the road and the guard rails and the lamp posts were still there somewhere, I could see nothing beyond the front of my car and it was a terribly eerie feeling, as though I had been swallowed in this thick fog and would never get out.

Shortly afterward, in the dark of an overnight flight back to England, those images and feelings came back very vividly, and they reminded me of the grief I was feeling about having just lost my father. Having bought a journal at the airport, just because it was very beautiful, I quietly rummaged through my bag, searching for it, and a pen, in the dark so as not to disturb the other passengers. The words were flooding into my head faster than I could write them down.

Upon returning home after the flight, I was surprised to find that it was actually quite legible, though it had been written with barely enough light to make out the outline of the journal cover!

This very short piece is what evolved from those notes that day...

Grief

As we walk along a road by night, there is a certain and undeniable beauty that comes with the dark. Quaint aging houses, well-tended gardens and hedgerows, ancient stone paths, grand oak trees which seem like wise old sages, all are appreciated as in the day, but each displays a different character by moonlight.

And so it is when we witness the various stages experienced by a loved one as he or she draws nearer to the final major event in life, an event as powerful and intimate as birth. We still see the character and beauty of the soul that inhabited the body, and gave us the precious gift and joy of loving relationship, while at the same time, we begin to see the flame of life flickering and fading, and both soul and body become beings we no longer know well.

To witness the process of the death of a loved one is to be violated by Grief. It descends upon us unwanted, unbidden, yet we are powerless to prevent its firm grasp on our souls. It is rather like walking a lonely, dark road on a clear, still night and finding ourselves in the midst of a dense fog. It doesn't always happen in an instant, just one moment in time; indeed, sometimes it creeps in slowly, giving only the most vague suggestions that it is lurking just ahead.

We walk that deserted, lonely road, dark and cold, so still and quiet, as the mist gently drifts from place to place, seeming innocuous enough as it plays hide and seek, yet it is unmistakably eerie, its intentions not at all harmless or playful. At first, it hangs in patches, giving us small tastes of it, allowing us to carry on, walking through it. Occasionally, it dances away from the face of the moon, and once again, the road is illuminated by a loving memory of the one we've lost.

But as it gathers itself, as the mist begins to hang thick with what seem to be ghosts, appearing, then vanishing, changing shape and form, we are suddenly in its grasp, seemingly out of nowhere. We lose our sense of direction and our hearts begin to fill with fear, panic at the thought that we won't find our way out of it. What was once a bright, full moon, casting its soft glow upon the land, lighting the way of the traveller as it gives new light and life to all it sees, becomes, instead, a dim spectre, shrouded in billowing mist. Where once, we could witness its quiet radiance illuminating cobblestone roads, sleeping blossoms, and whispering leaves, gradually, the mist engulfs them, keeping them secret in its ethereal quality.

Then we, too, become surrounded and consumed by it, as it keeps us feeling alone, cut off from all life, existing in a terrible, and terrifying place. We feel frozen in fear, immobilized and unable to move, unable to find our way out, unable to see that the quaint, aging houses, the well-tended gardens, the grand oak trees, the sleeping blossoms and the whispering leaves are still there, and know that they are just hidden in Grief. It is as though they, like the one we loved and lost, are gone from us forever, never to be seen or touched again. It is as though we, too, are gone, having been swallowed by it, becoming the ghosts that seem to live in the heavy mist that is Grief, appearing and vanishing, not quite of the Earth, unable to feel, to live -- becoming its undead.

Hope

Near the end of 2004, the year that I 'broke' and was in the thick of a major rebuilding of myself, I joined a wonderful website, FanArtReview.com. I began posting my art work, and reviewing beautiful creations of many other people. Having been very isolated, homesick and lonely in England for two years, I had suddenly found a wonderful community of friends with common interests.

I found a lot of laughter and giggles, and a lot of support and healing during my time at F.A.R., and have found some friendships that I know will last a lifetime. And to think that all I wanted was unbiased feedback about my art! The Universe gave me many gifts when I joined this wonderful group of people.

When I had to leave F.A.R. because I suddenly had an enormous amount of work to do, a book of art was created and dedicated to me by Pat Senior of Authors Incorporated, who received submissions from numerous people at F.A.R., as well as a few of my other friends and family members. I was overwhelmed by the response, and by the very beautiful messages that I received regarding my time at F.A.R. I struggled to find a way to thank everyone who contributed to the dedication book. Where does one begin with something like that?! This was such an honour, and I have found it impossible to express my gratitude to everyone who has been involved with it. This little story was written as my 'thank you' to my friends and to Pat Senior, my Angel, who together, created an incredible gift for me.

Hope

Once upon a time, a lost and broken little girl wandered through the Black Forest in a cold and lonely land, where the sun never rose. Stumbling through the woods, she was frequently pierced and scratched by branches and thorns that she could not see. Occasionally, the dim light of the moon, barely visible through the thick trees overhead, would cast just enough light for her to make her way through the brush, as she tried to find her way home.

One night, the little girl thought she heard the quietest ripples of laughter and giggles, and soft strains of cheerful music. She wondered if it was just a vague memory that was trying to surface, like when you wake from a dream, and recalling it seems just beyond your grasp.

She listened harder, shivering in the cold, and tried to follow the sounds, as she made her way through the dark forest. The laughter and music grew louder as she stumbled along, praying that she had found a way out, a way home.

After wandering for quite some time, to a part of the forest where she had never dared venture before, she suddenly came upon a clearing, filled with sunbeams pouring in from the Heavens. Having spent so much time in darkness, it was a blessing to see the light, yet it was so bright, she squinted against it, and held up her arms to shield her eyes.

She stood quietly hidden amongst the trees, peering through the branches, and before long, her eyes grew wide with wonder, as she peeked into this place which was far from the depths of the Black Forest. There, in the clearing, was a quaint little village full of elves and pixies, playing games, dancing, chasing each other and giggling. She heard beautiful, cheerful music, yet she could not determine its source. Everyone seemed to be having so much fun, and she longed to join in.

But she was lost and broken. They were not. They were elves and pixies. She was not. She hesitated, wondering whether she should make her presence known, when suddenly, one of the elves stopped his game of tag and stood straight and unmoving, as if he had heard a sound. Listening intently, he carefully began to search the surrounding trees with his eyes. Those around him also stopped what they were doing, as they noticed that he seemed to be searching for something.

Soon, he spotted the girl, hiding in the trees. "Look!" he cried. "There's another one!"

The little girl became frightened, not knowing what fate might befall her. She stood frozen, afraid to remain, but unable to run.

Suddenly, all eyes were upon her, as they followed the elf's gaze. Her fear mounted, her heart beating wildly in her chest. And just as suddenly, there were whoops and cheers, as they all rushed toward her, laughing and calling to her as they ran.

Realizing that she was being welcomed into their circle, her fear quickly dissolved into excitement, as she was embraced by this happy and playful little group. Gingerly making her way through the last of the sharp branches, she stepped into the beautiful sunlight, and closed her eyes as she bathed in its radiant glow, delighting in its warmth after being so long in the cold Black Forest.

Over the following days, the elves and pixies tended to her

wounds. They fed her, nourished her, coaxed and encouraged her to heal and to be well again. They taught her many things, and supported her constantly through her recovery. Little angels appeared now and then, quietly inspiring the friends, letting them know how to help the little girl, and she was told that they were responsible for the music that played continuously. It was their constant reminder to this little group that each one was special and loved by a Higher Power.

At first, it felt very strange to be so readily welcomed into this happy little village, but before long, it began to feel like Home. It did not take long for her to adjust to her new surroundings, and to adopt their ways and make them her own. Though it seemed strange at first, she quickly got used to their habit of feeding each other, rather than themselves. Days were spent playing and laughing. And at night, before they all settled in for a well-deserved rest, they gathered at the Brook of Wishes and Dreams and drank together. It was said that if they wished hard enough, all their dreams would come true.

Soon the little girl was thriving, happily laughing and playing with her new friends. She was certain that they had no idea what they had done for her, how many wounds they had healed, how much they had given her. She struggled to find the words to tell them 'thank you', to let them know what it meant to her to come from the cold, lonely Black Forest, and to be welcomed into this beautiful village and to find such wonderful friends, but the words never came. She only hoped that somehow, they knew what was in her heart.

One day, the little girl was playing with a couple of pixies near a pretty little pond. Giggling and chasing each other, they collapsed in laughter near its edge. The little girl was struck by how clear and perfect the water was, and she leaned over the edge to see if she could see the bottom of the pond.

Astonished, the reflection looking back up at her was that of a pixie! She did not know what to make of this; was this a magical pond, where pixies dwelt? She knew that pixies can be mischievous, and wondered if her little friends were simply playing with her. But as she formed the words to ask them the question, she saw that the pixie in the water seemed to be saying the same words.

Puzzled and bewildered, the little girl shook her head, and looked again at the reflection, pointing at it, and telling her friends to take a look. In a moment, as she peered into the water, seeing only the pixie's face, she also saw those of her friends next to it, as the three stared into the clear, cool water. She heard giggles beside her, as she struggled to make sense of this.

The three friends turned away from the pond, and the pixies explained that this place, far from anywhere, was a magical place, and that lost and broken children found healing there, becoming elves and pixies. No longer was she lost or broken. No longer was she different from them. They were all the same.

Not long after this revelation, the new little pixie was sitting by the Brook of Wishes and Dreams, alone except for the flowers, and the little animals that would sometimes come and sit with her for a while. Though she loved to play with her friends, she also enjoyed slipping away to spend some time daydreaming. It was fun to play "I wish, I dream", even though she knew those things would never come to pass.

She sprawled out on the cool, green grass in the shade of an old oak tree, and closed her eyes. Completely lost in her dreams, and having a wonderful time, a gentle little smile formed on her lips.

The new little pixie was so lost in thought that it took her a while to notice, through closed eyes, the bright glow that seemed to come from nowhere. From the depths of her daydreams, it finally occurred to her that lying in the shade, there should not be such a light. Opening her eyes, she saw an Angel, standing there in front of her, surrounded by a radiant light. She was very different from the sweet little angels who had wandered in and out of the village, checking on things, seeing to everyone's needs; this Angel was very beautiful, and it was obvious that she was also very powerful.

The little pixie sat up and rubbed her eyes, wondering if she had fallen asleep and was dreaming, yet the Angel did not vanish. Instead, she spoke to the pixie, telling her that all her wishes and dreams were about to be fulfilled. "Everything that you were just imagining will come true," said the Angel. "You will see. It will all become real very soon. But it will mean you have to leave your friends here."

The pixie was stunned. Her dreams would be fulfilled? How could this be so? Why would it happen to her? And why would she have to leave her friends? Bewildered, she asked the Angel these questions, but the only reply that came was a kind smile before she drifted skyward, disappearing into the bright sunlight, as the little pixie stared after her.

Sitting alone and astonished for some time, the little pixie could not understand what had happened. She spent some time trying to decide if the visit from the Angel had simply been a dream, incredulous at the notion that all her wishes would be fulfilled, and deeply saddened that it meant leaving her beautiful friends, and this wonderful place.

The little pixie stretched out on the grass again, and stared up at the clouds as they floated gently across the sky, considering all that the Angel had said, and what she needed to do. She struggled with the concept of leaving this place; it had been such a source of healing, support and laughter. She tried to imagine actually leaving, and saying goodbye, but then she remembered that they all sat together every night, drinking from the Brook of Wishes and Dreams, and realized that they would encourage her to follow her heart.

While the pixie lay in quiet contemplation of her future, the Angel made a very special appearance in the village, telling the pixie's friends what had happened, and asking them if they would like to do something wonderful for her. Her friends were overjoyed by the news of their friend's incredible luck. Immediately, they set about the task of preparing a very special celebration for her, wanting to surprise her upon her return from her daydreams.

And surprise her, they did! As the sun was beginning to set, the little pixie wandered back into the village, lost in thought about the impending changes in her life, and was stunned by what she saw. There, in the clearing, was the biggest celebration she had ever witnessed! An enormous banner was suspended from the arch of the gate with a congratulatory message for her. Vibrant streamers hung from trees and the cottages, and all the tables were covered with brightly coloured cloths, and a feast fit for a king. The entire village had been decorated with a stunning array of colours, shapes and patterns in a collection of beautiful works of art, which they had made themselves, and were dedicating to her.

She was so overwhelmed by these very loving gifts that she

stood, motionless and unable to speak, eyes wide and filling with tears. After a few moments, her friends noticed her there, at the edge of the clearing, and instantly, there were cheers, as they rushed toward her, telling her that the Senior Angel had told them her wonderful news, and had arranged this celebration of the occasion.

As they gathered excitedly around the little pixie with words of congratulations and well-wishing, some also told her how much they would miss her when she left. She was most surprised when many of her friends spoke of their sadness at her leaving, or of how much she had meant to them; she really did not expect to hear such kind words from most of the ones who shared their feelings. Some of them had written beautiful messages and poems for her, which they read to her at the party that evening. The little pixie was so overwhelmed by such an outpouring of support, friendship and love that she could only weep as her heart overflowed with appreciation for all that her friends and the Senior Angel had done for her.

During the celebration, the little pixie sat in a place of honour, which had also been beautifully decorated with her friends' creations. Her eyes wandered from table to table, each filled with the joyful faces of her friends, laughing and chatting amongst themselves over their feast, candles flickering in the evening breeze. She marvelled at the wonderful works of art that her friends had created, and the words they had written just for her. She contemplated the wishes and dreams that were about to be fulfilled, and could not believe that all of these incredible things could be happening to her.

But as wonderful as all the dreams would be when they came true, it was going to be very hard to leave this beautiful place. And once again, as she sat quietly, trying to drink it all in, she was so overcome with emotion that her eyes filled with tears. At that moment, the biggest, most powerful wish she had ever had rose up in her heart. She wished so hard that her wonderful friends and the Senior Angel could see all that she felt about them, about what they meant to her, about what they had done for her.

Just then, the Senior Angel drifted downward from the Heavens, lighting up the evening sky as if it were mid-day. All the chatter stopped, as everyone looked up, and watched as she floated silently until she stood in front of the little pixie, arms outstretched. The pixie rose and the Angel embraced her. Then holding the pixie away from her, she spoke so that all could hear.

"As you all know, your friend has wishes and dreams that are about to be fulfilled. But at this moment, she has one which is even more important than all the others."

She turned the pixie so that she was facing the crowd, the Angel standing behind her with her graceful hands on the tiny shoulders. And suddenly, the little pixie's chest began to glow. The light grew brighter and stronger, and all eyes were fixed upon it as it began to reach out, like little sunbeams that went directly from her heart to each of the hearts of her friends, and to the heart of the Senior Angel. When the light extended from the pixie to everyone else present, they all gasped as they found themselves feeling as though they were right inside her heart! Each one could feel her deep gratitude, appreciation and love for her friends and for the Senior Angel, and what they had done for her. It was a very magical moment for all present; no one had ever witnessed anything like it before.

After several moments, as tears fell from many eyes, and as everyone felt connected as never before, the light began to fade. The little pixie threw her arms around the Angel in a heartfelt embrace, trying to find words of gratitude, but she could find none that seemed adequate. The Angel simply smiled, and said that she already knew all that was unspoken.

After giving the friends a few moments to collect themselves, the Angel turned to the little pixie, and looking solemnly into her tiny face, she said, "Now, my dear, you must say your goodbyes. It is time."

The pixie turned back to her friends, and they all shared their final hugs, and a few quiet words. When the last goodbye had been spoken, the Senior Angel gathered the little pixie up in her arms and silently began to drift into the night sky, her radiant glow lighting their way.

Below them, all eyes watched, and all hands waved, until the light faded and the Angel could be seen no more. They were silent for a while, still looking Heavenward, trying to absorb all that had happened on this very magical day. Though they missed their little friend, they were happy to know that she was traveling to the Land of Wishes and Dreams. And as they quietly headed toward the Brook for their evening drink, they had renewed hope that one day, they would join her.

The Spirit Within

It was Wayne Dyer who said that we are not human beings having a spiritual experience, but rather, we are spiritual beings having a human experience. Long before I heard this simple, yet very powerful idea, it was what I believed.

How often we wonder what purpose or meaning there could be in our existence, in our struggles, in the tragedies and horrors of Life, and why some people seem to fare so much better than others. We say 'only the good die young', or we talk about 'bad things happening to good people'. We blame our hardships on God, or on others, or on ourselves, and spend a lifetime feeling resentful or remorseful. Some of us turn to a Higher Power in troubled times, while others of us turn away from it in anger.

This is the story of a little Spirit's journey before, during, and after the new Life and new Lessons that she chose. It offers an answer to the questions we have about our purpose on Earth, and gives an insightful Spiritual view of our Human existence. Undoubtedly, you will see some aspects of yourself in this book, as it speaks to many of our daily struggles, and to the importance of being spiritually connected. Because there are many common human struggles described and overcome in this story, it offers hope and healing to many.

Follow the Little Spirit's journey, and you will, in all likelihood, find yourself and some answers as you walk along with her.

The Spirit Within

The Keeper of the Stars was very busy. Indeed, there was always much to be done, as he tended these Mirrors of our Souls. It seemed that no sooner had he finished his duties with one Spirit, there was another coming to see him with Approval Documents and the accompanying Certificate Verifying Past Lives, watching as he put his spectacles on, and peered at the papers through wise, grey eyes. Having determined that the paperwork was in order, he would set about the task of carefully selecting a perfect, pure crystal star, which was befitting a Spirit as it began its chosen New Life.

There were times that the Keeper of the Stars could not help but smile to himself as he read the documents and saw what a Spirit has chosen for the Next Life, and Lessons to be Learned. Sometimes, the Spirits saw him gently shaking his head from side to side, his long white hair and beard moving back and forth as quiet little ripples on a summer pond. The younger ones had not yet learned to be unconcerned with the opinions of others. They often wondered just what the Old Man was thinking, but they were careful not to ask the question, for they knew he would never answer it.

The older ones paid no attention to what he may have thought of their choices, for they knew it mattered not at all. The Lessons were still required, whatever anyone's feelings about them might have been. The previous Lessons had taken immeasurable time and study; the preparation would not be wasted. They all knew when it was time, what needed to be done, and when they were ready to carry on.

And as that time drew nearer, a Spirit would often become restless, having taken as much time as was needed to absorb all the knowledge and information gained through previous Lives, and preparing for the challenges and Lessons in the next. With the new challenges identified, it was time to select a Life which would allow the best possible opportunities to face them, and to learn their Lessons.

And so it was that one day, a Spirit stood before God and Goddess, Creators and Parents of All Spirits, seeking approval for the New Life it had chosen. This Spirit, though very old, had regained, as a part of Lessons from previous Lives, much of its youthful and childlike quality. This always pleased God and Goddess, for they knew it meant Spirit was nearing completion of the Wheel of Learning. They smiled warmly when this sweet and gentle Spirit began to speak, for they heard an intriguing combination of Wise Old Soul, and Child Filled With Wonder, the best of all between the Beginning and the End.

They were not surprised when this Spirit requested a Life which would be fraught with great loss, much pain, and many difficult lessons, for they knew it was the next step required in the Progression of the Learning. Because they knew what was about to unfold, God and Goddess could not help but feel conflicted and protective of this Child of Theirs. As any parents, watching children grow and take steps which are necessary but will likely cause pain, God and Goddess felt some ambivalence, knowing of the heartache that this Child was about to endure, and wishing they could prevent the inevitable hurting.

However, as with many aspects of parenting, they knew it was entirely necessary to let go. It was meant to be exactly as it was going to unfold, and therein lay the deep respect and honour that came with knowing absolutely that it was well within the Child's ability. They were already eagerly anticipating watching as the Child moved through the next Life, enjoying many new experiences. As well, God and Goddess knew they would be patiently waiting for the Lessons to be learned, ready to be there to offer guidance and comfort when the harsh, cold Winds of Life would howl, as they slammed the Child Spirit into the rocks and stormy seas of Lessons needing to be learned. They looked forward to the day that their Child would return Home from the next Life, ready to receive the honours that would be due after much achievement and accomplishment.

The radiant little Spirit, eyes wide and bright, approached God and Goddess, who were seated on their thrones. They smiled warmly at this Spirit, standing there before them, and welcomed all who were present. The Angel in Charge of Proceedings sat behind his desk, shuffling papers and dipping a beautiful, feathery quill into an ink pot, as he began to prepare the necessary documents.

When everyone seemed ready to begin, Goddess spoke, her voice low and soothing. "You stand before us today, believing you have completed your current Study and Lessons, ready to choose your Next Life and continue on your Journey of Learning. We have been watching your progress since the Beginning of Time, and we are most pleased with all you have learned."

Spirit was beaming, delighted with such an acknowledgement.

Goddess continued. "You have had many Lives, and have become very wise through your mistakes, your experience and your diligent studies. Of course, your Lessons grow more difficult with each New Life, as you become increasingly capable of handling such challenges. Tell us, please, about the New Life and the Lessons you have chosen, beginning with the foundation for them, which you so carefully laid in your Past Lives."

Spirit needed no encouragement to begin, clearly outlining Past Life experience and learning, as well as the chosen New Life, and Lessons that it was hoped would be mastered. It was most certainly going to be a long and arduous journey, but Spirit was not afraid. Rather, the telling of the Life and the expected Lessons was delivered with much conviction and enthusiasm, and with a strength that seemed contradictory to the gentle sweetness of this childlike Spirit.

Occasionally, God and Goddess smiled knowingly at each other, nodding gently, confirming their understanding of, and agreement with all that they heard. It was not their habit to interrupt or to ask questions during these orations; it was essential that each Spirit be allowed to speak until there were no more words, so that God and Goddess could make a proper assessment, based purely on what had come from a Spirit's own pondering and learning, and not altered by any hint or suggestion that they may have given.

At the conclusion of the lengthy disquisition, the little Spirit drew a long breath, and letting it out slowly, stood quietly, waiting. God and Goddess had been most impressed by what they had heard, and needed no time between them to grant their approval.

"Once again, you have been diligent in your studies, and have proven yourself to be well-prepared for the challenges which you have so eloquently described," said the Goddess.

"Indeed," added God. "We have no doubt that you will succeed in this Life, and in these Lessons, and that you will return Home to us with an even deeper understanding of

The Greater Plan. We will be watching you, Child. You will not be alone on your Journey. Go now, with our blessing."

The little Spirit ran to her Parents and the three shared a warm embrace, knowing it would be their last for a very long time.

The Angel in Charge of Proceedings had been listening intently to this shy little Spirit, and felt a tugging at his heart when he heard the lengthy list of Lessons that were to be tackled in the New Life. The Angel looked somewhat dubious, despite the fact that he had witnessed countless such appeals since The Beginning of Time, and despite the fact that this particular Spirit truly seemed to have got all the homework done, and was as prepared as any he had ever seen. The previous Lessons all fit, the analysis was thorough and the delivery was exceptional. But the uneasiness within him grew. He did not often get too involved with the Spirits when they made these applications, but something about this one was different. He supposed it was the quiet, childlike manner of this Spirit, which made him question whether the New Life was going to be overwhelming. He feared that for this gentle little Soul who stood before God and Goddess on this particular day, it would, on some other day, be that way.

His heart skipped a beat when approval was given, and he was asked to fill out the necessary documents. His doubtful expression quietly changed to one of concern, which he tried to cover with a nervous smile, as the Spirit left the embrace and hurried to his desk to collect the papers. Hiding his feelings, he handed the completed paperwork to the excited little Spirit, who thanked him and skipped off to see the Keeper of the Stars.

When he was certain he would not be overheard, the Angel

approached the God and Goddess. "Begging your pardon, I know I have no right to question your judgement, but with all due respect, I must speak. Did you not see the many places along that path that this Spirit was in danger of returning too soon? There were too many breaking points. That Life is like a porcelain plate, exceptionally thin in many places. A tiny tap in just a certain way, at a certain moment, and it will shatter."

Both God and Goddess listened carefully to the Angel's concerns, then Goddess gathered her silver gown about her, and rose from her throne of moss, leaves and flowers. Smiling as she approached the Angel, she stretched out her hands to take his, seeing his fear and worry, and wanting only to reassure him.

"You will see," she said, with the utmost confidence, as she looked directly into his eyes. "There are many potential breaking points in that Life, yes. But this Spirit has a strength and a will that will fortify and protect it from all of that. Do not be fooled by such a childlike appearance; there is great strength and wisdom in that Spirit. I agree, it does seem a lot for one Life. And there will, indeed, be many times when Spirit is balancing rather precariously along potentially lethal cliffs. But I believe that it will be purposeful. This Spirit will overcome those rocks and storms, and will surprise many. You will see. You must trust."

"But Goddess," the Angel replied, "We know that sometimes the Lives are not completed in the way everyone hoped, or the way the Spirit planned. You know that it is always risky when Spirits choose the Lesson of Finding Strength Versus Giving Up. It is one of the hardest Lessons, and the Spirits do not always master it, as they thought they would. Sometimes, that Lesson overwhelms the Spirits, and they choose to come Home before it is time. They do not realize that they will merely have to repeat the Lesson; it is such a waste, so much suffering for nothing."

Goddess took one of the Angel's hands in both of hers and held it tightly. "You know it is never 'for nothing'. And it is never 'before it is time'," she reminded him. "We know that some things are Meant To Be. And we know the Spirits have Free Will. They all make the best choices they can based on the circumstances in which they have put themselves, whether it is in the choosing of their New Lives, or in the living of them. We must trust that it will all turn out for the best, which people commonly mistake for meaning that things will turn out the way they want them to do. But that is not the case. All conditions of The Lives serve a Higher Purpose; they are all part of the Greater Plan. The Lessons must be taught in the best possible way for each Spirit to learn. You must trust that everything that happens is for the highest possible good, no matter how it may look on the surface."

She was right; he did know these things, and he knew them well. Yet this time, something felt different. The Angel's fears were not at all relieved. The Goddess could not reassure him that the little Spirit would be all right in the New Life; she could only tell him that he must accept whatever happens as being the best possible outcome. He could feel his anxiety begin to grow, as he watched the Spirit skipping off into the distance, paperwork in hand, the wheels now set in motion, beginning what felt to the Angel like an ominous chain of events.

The little Spirit needed no reminders to find the Keeper of the Stars, having had countless Lives before this one, and knowing well how to find the Old Man. He heard the little footsteps approaching, and turned to greet the excited Spirit. "Ah, welcome!" he exclaimed. "How delightful to see you once again! It has been a very long time; you must have been studying very earnestly since your last Life."

"Yes, indeed, Sir," was the serious reply, as Spirit handed the papers to him.

"Please, do sit down," he offered, as he gestured toward a chair. "Let me see now..." he said, as he squinted and peered through his spectacles at the first page. As he read, he sank into a very large old chair and immediately, it was apparent that all his concentration was directed to the contents of the documents.

Spirit obediently sat, and waited as he carefully read every word. His was not an easy task. He had to carefully consider all that had been learned in Previous Lives, along with what was expected in the New Life, and decide how large the crystal star must be in order for it to fulfill its role.

Spirit watched his face as he read all the relevant information, his eyebrows occasionally rising together, as if in surprise, or one at a time, as if in concern. Occasionally, he stroked his long beard thoughtfully as he read, and finally, he put down the pile of papers, laid his spectacles on top of them, and looked at the little Spirit, sitting so quietly and patiently in front of him. With a warm and loving look, he said, "I have just the perfect piece of crystal for you. I have been watching you since The Beginning of Time, and have been waiting for the day when it would mirror your essence. Come along; let me show you!"

With that, the Old Man guided Spirit through the Heavens, and as he did so, Spirit wondered about the star that he had decided would be representative of the Lessons of the New Life, reflecting the continuing journey of such an Old Soul and mirroring its essence. Though it would begin as a perfectly clear crystal star, over time, as wounds were inflicted on the Spirit, it would be cut, scratched, chipped and broken.

As well, each time Spirit wounded another, the star would also be marred three times more, for what we put out into the Universe will come back to us threefold. It is not only a sin against another, but also against one's own Spirit to cause harm in any way. It goes against all that is good and right and just.

However, not all that happened to the crystal stars was hurtful, for they were able to repair some of the damage done to them. Given that the stars were reflections of Souls, when the Spirits performed selfless and loving deeds, or experienced anything which was of a healing nature to them, not only were pieces of the Soul restored, but so were pieces of the crystal.

After drifting through the Heavens together, the two arrived at an immense, flawless and incredibly brilliant crystal star. It was so beautiful, in fact, the humble Spirit could only weep, for there were no words to describe how it felt to have oneself compared with such perfection.

Spirit turned to the Old Man and threw her arms around him, as a child hugging a father. As they held each other for a moment, there were quiet words of farewell between them.

The Old Man stood for a while, a wise and knowing look on his kind and lovely face, those beautiful grey eyes, watching and waiting for the moment Spirit would be ready for the next step.

And finally, it came. Spirit drifted toward the crystal, pausing immediately in front of it just long enough to turn and give a loving look of respect and appreciation to the Old Man.

On turning back to face the star, the Spirit suddenly began to glow, becoming a bright, radiant energy, engulfing the star, swirling faster and faster, and passing right through it, charging it with Spirit's energy, the crystal becoming so brilliant, it was difficult for the Keeper of the Stars to keep his gaze upon it. Suddenly, after one explosive flash, Spirit vanished, having gone to inhabit the tiny being that would manifest it on the physical plane. The crystal star, suspended in its place in the dark skies, had finally begun to fulfill its purpose. The Old Man awaited the day, some long years down the road, when its role would be completed, and it would illuminate the Heavens.

And so began Spirit's New Life as a little girl. Her earliest consciousness, which was, of course, at the same moment she entered her physical being, was that of feeling unloved and unwanted. 'Ah,' she thought to herself, 'I remember choosing this Lesson'. How tragic that she was merely one new cell, supposedly safe inside her mother's womb, and already, she felt lost and threatened, knowing that she had chosen parents who were young and unable to care for her, and who would contemplate tearing this tiny scrap of life from the mother's body, thus immediately filling the little Spirit with fear for her very survival. And the irony of it was that in feeling unloved and unwanted by the people upon whom she relied to keep her safe and protected, the seeds of self-destruction were sewn. It was a powerful imprinting of the belief system which went to the core of the child; she had no value and did not deserve to exist. The battle had begun: her instinctive will to live versus her belief that she should die. It was a battle that would not soon end.

All of this happened in a flash, as Spirit entered the single cell which would one day become a little girl who lived in a frightening, hostile environment, and she recognized that the Lessons had begun. And in the same moment, far away in the silent sky, a tiny piece of the beautiful crystal shattered. The Keeper of the Stars was still standing next to it, Spirit having vanished just an instant before, and upon witnessing this heartbreaking sight, a heavy tear rolled quietly down his soft cheek.

With each passing day, as with every Life before, the memories of the Spirit World and the reasons why she chose this Life were fading, and Spirit realized that her humanness was taking over, as it needed to do. She likened it to falling asleep, albeit for a rather long time in some Lives. But even in sleep, one is still somewhat aware of one's surroundings. Spirit would still be present, but overshadowed by the Human element, which had to be strong in order to allow Spirit to have the Human experience. This would ultimately lead her to the required learning, if she managed to stay on her chosen path. Eventually, the Spirit would awaken, and then...well, then things would be different.

Before long, while still a tiny Human, all conscious memory of Spirit Life disappeared, and the little girl was left to begin her difficult journey, feeling all alone and frightened.

The Keeper of the Stars well knew what was happening to the little girl, though he never saw her physical being at all while she was in her New Life. It was, of course, because the Old Man, as he wandered through the Heavens, tending to the needs of the stars, would pass by her beautiful crystal 'mirror', and could see what was happening. Though it did not surprise him, having read her Application, it was heartbreaking to see steadily worsening damage to the beautiful crystal. He understood how it all worked; he well knew about the Lessons and the Greater Plan, and what is Meant To Be...But in all his years doing this work, all that knowledge never made it easier to see damage to the Spirits beginning to show in the precious crystal stars as they hung quietly in the dark sky, waiting.

The time came for the little girl to enter the world as a separate little person, setting out on the journey that was her new Life. The Human parents who had provided the body for this little Spirit were very young, still really children themselves, and therefore, were unable to give the child the kind of love that allows a child to thrive. Their own journeys were exceptionally painful and difficult as well, and although it was not their intention, the little girl had been brought into an environment that was cold, lonely and hostile. She was already imprinted with the belief that she was unloved, unwanted, unimportant. Already, she had learned that to be loved meant that she was helpless and powerless. Already, she had learned that the people who were meant to love and care for her were people who created a need for her to fear for her safety, themes that would be re-created again and again in this Life.

And so she was set on a course of trying to learn the truth about Perfect Love, Perfect Trust, and Perfect Acceptance. But it would be many long and painful years until these Truths were shown to her.

The young parents had their own challenges and Lessons to learn, and theirs were, of course, connected to those of the little girl. They had been chosen for many reasons, reasons that the Spirit knew when she was preparing for this Life, but which were unbeknownst to the child. Their role was to provide an Earthly form for the Spirit, and to lay the groundwork for the Lessons that she was required to learn. But these people were not destined to see the girl, or her two brothers who came later, through to adulthood. The

Parents, young and frightened, were ill-equipped for parenting, though they did their best with the task during the time that they had been given to try.

In time, the Father's Lessons took him to a terrible place, the kind that the Human experience does not understand, but it was of the kind that God, Goddess and the Spirits knew were Meant To Be. And in that terrible place, the father killed his wife, and then himself, his young children watching in horror, their innocence violently torn from them in that moment. Though the Spirits of all who were involved knew it was part of The Greater Plan, those on Earth who were a part of it, or who were affected by it, could not begin to comprehend such actions.

Living separately from her brothers, the little girl was placed with her Earthly Family, where she had hoped to find healing and happiness. Yet it was not meant to be. Rather, she found confirmation of her previous learning, that love means violation, judgement, rejection and betrayal. Most of the people closest to the child were very young Spirits, and from conception onward, she was subjected to their soul-murdering behaviour. The seeds of the Lessons had long since been sewn. And in toxic soil, they had taken root and would continue to grow. Although she was unaware of Spirit moving inside her, it was there, urging her to carry on, in the hopes that someday, the Lessons which were to come from this situation would be learned, and true healing would finally be found.

To help her to master these Lessons, it was essential that the little girl should be closely connected with very young Spirits. In the selection of this Life and its Lessons, she chose a Mother and Brothers in her second family who were, indeed, very wounded themselves. As a result, the Mother was destined to be the best teacher the little girl could have had, with the Brothers compounding everything the girl would learn from her.

The connection between the girl and the Mother was, in that regard, a perfect spiritual relationship. But for the little girl, and later for the woman, it was also one of the greatest sources of ongoing pain in her Human Life. The damage was so deep that The Old Man frequently heard the soft tinkling of glass breaking, as piece by piece, the crystal was almost completely shattered.

The girl endured unending abuse from the Mother, ceaseless insults and shaming words. The harsh and unnecessary judgements and criticisms were relentless, and once they had taken a firm hold in the little girl's mind, and in her Soul, the Mother did not even need to say them any more. The girl had absorbed the Mother's beliefs into every cell, and once those beliefs were integrated into her Soul, it was exceptionally difficult to begin to undo the damage, to change the beliefs, and to heal the terrible scars. This undoing was going to be one of the Spirit's hardest Lessons.

The Brothers were very physically and emotionally violent with the girl, seeming to delight in causing her pain.

The Father, though loving and gentle with the child, was absent much of the girl's life. She often wondered why he could not be there more often to protect her. Home and family should have been safe and comforting; however, for the girl, there was only fear. But she had chosen this Mother, these Brothers, this family, for many reasons. It was years before she understood that it needed to be that way in order for her to learn the Lessons she had chosen for this Life. All of this was part of The Greater Plan; all of it was Meant To Be.

Despite the physical and emotional violence in her family,

the girl trusted her parents to do what was best for her, and believed that they loved her. This was all she had known, from the moment of her conception, and in both families. It was only natural for a child to trust her parents, and to need to believe she was loved by them. From the beginning of her existence in this Life, she had learned that love meant fear; it was as simple as that.

The girl grew into a woman, and the trusting continued, not just with the Mother, but with many other people. From childhood, she learned that she was expected to give up her power and control to anyone who wanted them, or risk more danger. Therefore, as she grew to become a woman, she kept connecting herself with people who validated those beliefs, reinforcing the learning that love means painfully giving up the Self.

These relationships did not begin this way, however; at least, not on the surface. In the early days, it would always be the same... words of flattery, words of need, words of love. Always, these men seemed to know just what the woman needed to hear. So easily, they spoke those words, with as much passion and conviction as it took to make her believe them. And because of her desperate need to be loved and wanted, so easily, she did.

Once she was hooked, the abuse and rejection began, always slowly and quietly at first, but just enough to play on her fear of being abandoned and unloved, which ran through to her very soul. In response to this fear, she would try harder to please, to be loved, and so the cycle would continue, eventually becoming a downward spiral, spinning out of control, seemingly unending. The more abuse and rejection she endured, the more she tried to be worthy of being loved. It was eating her alive.

The woman's unhealthy relationships extended beyond the

men with whom she became involved; she found the same themes repeated in every area of her Life. Often, with her friendships, and even when she became a mother, she found that she was so desperately searching for love, that she was willing to give up her Self to find it.

With such a toxic foundation at the core of all of these relationships, she was doomed to be miserable.

Time and time again, she was puzzled, even bewildered by the fact that no matter what she did, she could not find peaceful and loving relationships. She struggled to understand why it always went wrong, why it always meant fear, and repeated attempts to break her Spirit. She kept fighting to make things better, though her attempts were futile. She knew something was wrong, she knew something was missing, but the knowledge of it seemed always to be just beyond her grasp. Although she was unaware, her desire to understand meant Spirit was moving inside her, urging her to continue her search for Perfect Love, Perfect Trust, and Perfect Acceptance.

There were times the woman was nearly beaten, so close to defeat that she almost proved the Angel right, almost choosing to give up, rather than learn the Lesson of Finding True Strength. But something always pulled her back from the edge. It took her many years to understand what that something was, and it did not come all at once. The countless painful bits and pieces of the woman's Life had to be put together like a long and miserable puzzle before Spirit was finally allowed to peek through and illuminate the dismal human existence that had been chosen so long ago for the Higher Purpose. It was then, when Spirit finally reached out and connected with the woman, that the healing was about to begin.

Of course, the woman had always been unaware of Spirit's

presence in her life, moving quietly, sustaining her, feeding her, even when she thought she would break. It was Spirit, who had been the source of the woman's strength, allowing her to endure her long and difficult struggles. Without it, they would have completely destroyed her, thereby making the Angel's words become prophecy rather than simple concern. But then came the turning point. It was time to begin the deepest healing, and it would not be an easy path. Although that strength had served her well, Spirit knew it was time to show the woman that it was no longer a tool to help her endure; rather, it had become her destroyer. Her Lifelong Protector had become her Killer.

This Lesson proved to be extremely difficult for the woman in a way that the others had not. Her strength had woven itself into the very heart of her identity. She had worn it like a badge of honour. She, and all who knew her, had come to rely on this as an integral part of who she was. It terrified her to imagine what others would think of her if she were anything but Always The Strong One. And probably, most frightening of all was how it would alter her opinion of herself. She had always known herself so well, but she did not know who she would be at the end of the shedding of this self-destructive identity. The badge of honour had grown into a suit of armour, which was keeping her isolated not only from others, but from herself. It had cut off her ability to be all she was meant to be. It was keeping her from fully sharing and experiencing her Life, and her Self.

Somehow, she had to find a different kind of strength, the kind that would allow her to be weak, to need, to lean, to be dependent upon others. History had taught her of the danger in these, so it came as no surprise that she found herself facing a terrifying fork in the road. It seemed to her as though either of the two paths presented would be the death of her.

And in fact, this was quite true. She stood at the fork and gazed upon the Road of Familiarity, so dry and barren, brown and lifeless, knowing that Death stood waiting for her at the end of it. And as she peered cautiously down the Road of Change, she could see that it was overgrown with branches, lush and thick with leaves, hanging over the path, making it dark and impossible to see what was beyond the first bend. Her heart skipped a beat, and she was filled with fear, for Death stood waiting at the beginning of that road. To begin the journey along that path meant the Death of the Self she had come to know so well. Although she was aware that Re-Birth awaited her just beyond, this was very frightening. She only knew how to be strong and independent. It seemed inconceivable to her that she was deserving of the permission to also be weak, to be vulnerable, to need, since these had only yielded anger or rejection from others. She knew she had to find a balance between strength and weakness, that there was room for both, which would allow her to be a whole person with the frailties that she had always allowed others, but never herself.

She stood and pondered the two paths, fearful of travelling both. Contemplating the consequences of each journey, she seemed to move toward the Road of Familiarity, which seemed much less frightening than the Road of Change. Suddenly, Spirit burst forth, showing her that if she gave Fear her power, and refused to walk the new and terrifying path, she would die.

And so, with one small and hesitant step, she chose Life, and gingerly set out to find it.

For many long years, the Keeper of the Stars had wandered through the Heavens, past that incredible crystal star, watching in silent horror as the wounds appeared on it, one after another, after another. He remembered the gentle

104

sweetness of the Spirit, the quiet strength which was truly remarkable, and the courage, which was well-hidden behind the innocence. Many times, he leaned against that once-perfect crystal star, and wept, his tears falling onto the crystal and dulling its formerly brilliant finish. He was certain that the Spirit would not be defeated, and that one day, there would be a radiant star in the Heavens, the likes of which were seldom seen. But in the meantime, he was well aware of the suffering that was taking place in the little Spirit's Life. He could do nothing but wait for the turn-around he knew would come. And finally, that day had arrived.

Spirit led the woman down the Road of Change, gaining in strength as the woman's journey of healing began. Slowly, some of the cracks, scratches and chips on the crystal began to disappear. It was a long and difficult process, but the woman kept working at it. The journey was not without its pitfalls, and there were times when it seemed as though the woman had not really learned the Lessons at all, falling back into the Old Ways, but still, she persevered. Although at times, it was one step forward, two steps backward, she carried on, Spirit taking the woman's hand and leading her on her healing journey. As the woman remembered and relied on Spirit, the human element faded, giving way to her true essence, allowing her to find her Self.

God and Goddess were, of course, watching every step of the way, and they were delighted to see that this Child of Theirs had finally reached this point. They smiled lovingly at each other, and at the woman, knowing that when she returned to them, she would be relating wonderful and powerful Lessons that had been learned.

When Earthly Lives were completed, and the Spirits had returned Home, they were met by the Keeper of the Stars, and by God and Goddess. They were expected to give an accounting of some of what they had learned, as well as the meaning of the wounds on their crystal stars. When the damage was caused by another, it would be repaired with healing and forgiveness. And when the damage was due to wounds inflicted on another, three things were required in order for it to be healed: Understanding of the consequences of the Spirit's actions, remorse and asking forgiveness for the pain that was caused, and forgiveness received.

It was also expected that these incidents would be the cause of much reflection and contemplation, as Spirits prepared to repeat the Lesson, and to learn many others in their Next Lives.

It was usually a rather gruelling exercise for the younger Spirits, who had to accept responsibility for having chosen not to learn all of their Lessons. But when they were all finished, when they had made the last acknowledgement and heartfelt apology, when they had finally come to understand the consequences of their actions, they would once again become swirling energy, surrounding and inhabiting their crystal stars, finally allowing them to shine in the Heavens, contemplating all they had mastered, and all that was yet to be learned.

The glow emanating from each of the stars was directly proportionate to the size of the crystals, to the imperfections remaining on them, and ultimately, to the Lessons learned by the Spirits through all their Lives. The youngest Souls, who had learned the fewest lessons, had usually seriously wounded other Spirits; therefore, their stars were small and did not shine very brightly. But one day, they would again be given the chance to progress, when they had done all the study and preparation necessary to leave the crystal, and seek further growth by choosing a New Life.

And so it was that one day, the Mother died, and like all other Spirits, she was led to the Meeting with the Keeper of the Stars, and with God and Goddess, who were seated next to her crystal star. It was the usual practice during these Meetings that God and Goddess did not speak, for they did not wish to interfere with the flow of thought, and given that this was, in fact, like a test, they did not wish to give away any answers. They would always sit in silence, and let the Spirits speak until they were through.

The Mother stood before them, and was asked to go through the innumerable wounds on her crystal. It was so damaged, it was almost impossible to find any clear, untouched space on it. The Mother spoke of her journey, her troubles, and of the many wounds which had been inflicted on her. Hers was such a young Spirit that even being back Home, she had trouble understanding what had happened in her Earthly Life. Very quickly, it became evident that she was locked in the Human Life, and that she was struggling to reconnect with her Spirit, a struggle which had been apparent during her time on Earth, and one which had not been mastered.

Although it was difficult to understand from a Human perspective, this Spirit was playing a necessary role in the Greater Plan. The Daughter Spirit needed the Mother Spirit to be this way, or she would not have mastered as many of her Lessons as she needed to do in that Life. In this regard, even the youngest, least developed, and seemingly most destructive Souls still managed to be teachers.

However, within the Greater Plan, which required certain Things Meant To Be, there was also room for Free Will. There were always opportunities for the Spirits to choose to learn or to reject some of their Lessons. The Old Man, God and Goddess well understood that although many of the

Mother's Lessons were not meant to be fully learned in this Life, she had chosen to ignore opportunities for some of her learning. It had been possible for her to fulfill her role in each of the lives of many Spirits, working with the Greater Plan, yet still mastering even a few of her own Lessons without upsetting the balance, but she had not done so and would have to repeat those Lessons in the future.

In her Earthly Life, the Mother's need for power and control had been motivated by insecurity, and her fear that she would be alone and unloved. In the Spirit world, all could see the irony in this, but in the Earthly realm, so many Humans suffered from the same fear, yet only the Oldest Souls knew how to overcome it. The answer came only after having had many Lives, and learning many Lessons.

The Mother stood before the Old Man, the God and the Goddess, stumbling over her words as she attempted to reconnect with her Spirit. It was a lengthy and difficult Meeting, going through each of the wounds on her crystal. At first, she was extremely defensive, refusing to take responsibility for any of the pain she had inflicted on others, and therefore, on herself, as well. Some allowance had been made for the wounds which had been inflicted by others on her own Spirit, but still, she had chosen her Life and her Lessons, and although she was not intended to master many, she had not made as much progress as had been possible. Clearly, this Spirit would need to do a great deal of studying before being ready or able to seek approval for another Life.

As with the youngest Spirits, she had been reluctant to let go of her Human form until the last possible moment, preferring to stay connected with the Earthly Realm, rather than to reconnect with her Higher Self. Finally, as she neared the completion of the accounting of her Life, the

Mother Spirit began to let go of the look of the Human body it had inhabited for so long, and as she did so, some of the Lessons came to her. She began to remember why she had chosen that particular Life. She had a better understanding of all that had taken place, of the wounds she had endured, of how they had affected her. She forgave those who had hurt her throughout her Life, and soon realized how much damage her own wounds had caused others, damage for which she sought Forgiveness. And finally, she saw the places where she could have progressed but had chosen not to do so, promising to consider those before her next Life.

The Keeper of the Stars was delighted when the Mother Spirit had reached this point, for her crystal was beginning to repair itself, and before the eyes of all who stood nearby, its clarity and brilliance were beginning to return.

The Mother's accounting now complete, she turned to her crystal star. With one long, last look at God, Goddess and the Keeper of the Stars, she smiled, knowing that they loved her still. She stood, gazing at them, losing any last trace of her Earthly form, returning again to Pure Spirit. Slowly, she began to swirl and spin, charging the crystal with her energy. Though it was not one of the largest or most radiant stars in the Heavens, there had been enough healing of the Mother's wounds, and enough understanding of her Lessons, that the crystal had been sufficiently repaired to produce a soft and gentle glow.

And it remained that way, unchanged for some years, until the day that the Daughter returned Home to God and Goddess, her true Parents, and stood facing them and the Keeper of the Stars for her reckoning. She always likened that part of the Homecoming to a final exam after many years' worth of study and learning.

With outstretched arms, God and Goddess welcomed the Spirit, eager to embrace their Child after her long journey. After a few moments' silence, all simply enjoying being together again, it was Spirit who was the first to speak. She was barely able to contain many of the Lessons which had been learned while living the Life of the tormented little girl who grew into the damaged woman, and who then had become a woman who healed, both her Self and others. Standing there in the presence of God, Goddess, and the Keeper of the Stars, she still bore the shape and the face of that woman, as Spirits always did when they first arrived back Home, still connected to their Human experience on the Earthly Plane.

She spoke of the loneliness at first, since this was the first consciousness she had experienced in this Life. "I was so lost," she said. "I didn't belong anywhere. I felt as though I was not loved, and my very survival was threatened right from the first moment. It was as if I had been cut off, even from myself. I was all wrong. These themes continued through my childhood and well into my adult Life. Of course, I did not remember my past Lives, so I had no idea why I continually ended up in situations which only served to confirm those beliefs, and which threatened my life and my Soul."

It seemed as though the thoughts were bubbling up inside, spilling forth in words she could no longer contain. She had the attention of the Old Man, as well as her Creators, as she continued with excitement. "In this Life, I chose four parents, each of whom would contribute in various ways to the learning I was ultimately meant to do. Some taught me that I was not allowed to have any control or feelings, that I was unimportant to anyone. I was stripped of my ability to express myself, and I was criticized, insulted and shamed daily. I was expected to be dutiful and obedient, and was considered unacceptable as myself. I was told I did not deserve good things, and I was subjected to a lot of violence, and violation. I was not safe or protected.

"The second father I had chosen also contributed to the difficulties I had, though it was mostly by way of his inability to protect me from what was going on around me. Of course, eventually, I came to realize that it was meant to be that way, but as a child, it was a very painful and unanswered question to me. He was, however, very loving at times, but I did not notice it for many long years because of the overwhelming negativity surrounding me. Any good he was able to do was overshadowed, outweighed, suffocated by the toxic black cloud that was swallowing my very Soul."

Her eyes misted, and she recalled the human experience of being a daughter whose father died.

God and Goddess looked knowingly at one another, remembering how she relied on them during the last days of the Father's Life. They well-remembered the Daughter's struggles of Human experience versus Spiritual being throughout that period. They heard her pleas for strength; they heard her confusion, asking for the Father to be taken, to stop his suffering; and then they heard her acknowledge knowing that to ask this was taking away the Father's Free Will. At some points, through her loving tears, she said she no longer cared about that; the Father hurt so much, she just wanted it to stop. She said she wanted to pray like other people and just ask for him to be taken to the Other Side. But always, she immediately recanted, knowing that it was wrong to attempt to alter the course of one of the most important events in the Father's own Life and Lessons, and knowing that it would ultimately alter hers, as well, if she did that.

Instead, she pondered what she was meant to learn from

this difficult experience, remembering that this Human event was another opportunity for Spiritual growth. She continued to ask for strength to get through it all, and she asked to be allowed to be with the Father when he crossed over, since he had indicated to the Daughter that this was his wish.

The Old Man thought back to that time, and remembered how the crystal star was cracking like never before, and how suddenly, very late one night, a huge piece of it shattered, sending tiny shards flying in several directions. It was the moment the Daughter, who had been diligently watching the rise and fall of her Father's chest, heard the escape of one long last breath and realized there would not be another.

Indeed, it had been one of the most difficult times in the woman's Life, but it was because she loved her Father so. Though she had struggles with him in her Life, the two of them had long since made peace and all had been forgiven. Although she knew that someday, they would meet again on the Other Side, she knew she was going to miss his physical presence, being held in the warm embrace of her Father's arms, feeling the love that was in her Father's smile. She also realized that the amount of pain she experienced was equal to the amount of love that was felt, and in that knowledge, was content to bear the hurt of losing her beloved Father. He was the only one who fed the girl's starving Soul at all during the darkest times of her young life. And for much of the rest of the time they had together, it had been the same.

She used to wonder why the Father had been unable to keep her safe from the Mother and the Brothers, but after a time, she came to understand that she had chosen it to be this way for many reasons. Part of the Spiritual Lesson was about standing up for herself. But this was one of the longest and hardest battles she had. It was a Lesson which was learned a wee bit at a time, in little steps over a very long period. It would have been impossible for her make any progress in this, had there always been someone there, protecting her.

The Spirit continued. "This family also gave me the opportunity to work on Self-worth and Self-love. I struggled with these Lessons for a very long time, and they were among the most difficult. It should not be so hard to love the Self, given that it is so easy to love and value others. It is one of the most essential elements to living a happy and healthy Human Life. Without truly loving and honouring the Self, the Human Life suffers physically, mentally, and emotionally, because it is actually a Spiritual condition of starvation and of withering. And that is where I lived for much of this Life, unable to feel the kind of love and respect for my Self that I felt for others.

"For many years, I thought that my struggle with this was a purely Human one, that my Human Self had been so deeply wounded after repeatedly being given messages about my not being valuable, lovable, deserving of anything good. After a time, I came to believe that it was a Human problem that could be remedied in the Spiritual realm.

"But one day, I was struck by the most profound insight. I understood that it was not my Human Self that was wounded, or carrying the pain; it was my Spirit, and it needed healing. It was a much deeper injury than I had ever imagined. I had always thought that all the pain we experienced as Humans was simply on that level, wounding us emotionally, and that all the hurts of an Earthly Life could be healed by connecting with our Spiritual selves. But I was wrong.

"In that Life, I remember thinking that we choose our

Earthly Lives and our Lessons before we inhabit a body, and are meant to learn and grow as Spirits. I thought of all Human experience as contributing to Spiritual Lessons, and sought to find the lesson in the difficult parts of my Earthly Life. It took many years, and many terrible times before I understood that as Spirits, we, too, can be wounded, battered, and sometimes in a sense, even killed.

"When Human troubles flare, a person will often seek guidance and strength by turning to a Spiritual Source outside himself. He does not understand that in reality, he is reconnecting with his own Spirit, which is the true source of healing. It is true that You, our True Parents, God and Goddess who created us, are always here for us, but it is not the two of You who do the healing work or provide the strength we need in our Earthly Lives. Your role is to show us Perfect Love, teaching it by your example. It is that Love which sustains us, as Human and Spirit work together to heal the Self.

"However, there are times when the wounds are too deep, and Spirit is well hidden, seemingly out of reach. The Soul is beaten and bruised, and a profound healing of the Spirit is necessary. If it does not happen, the physical body will become sick and die, for it manifests all that is the Spirit. It is Spirit which gives Life and Energy, and it is Spirit which takes them away.

"How often do we listen to Humans say 'The body is not really the person, it is the Spirit or the Soul that defines him or her'? They say the body is just a vessel to contain the Spirit, a means by which the Spirit fulfills its purpose. We especially hear them say such things when they are contemplating death. And to an extent, they are correct.

"However, they are missing a vitally important point. The body is so much more than a mechanical vessel; every cell becomes empowered by the Spirit, by the Life Force. It is a perfect marriage of the physical and the Spiritual, the deepest kind of interconnectedness possible. One cannot exist without the other. It is like a Perfect Circle of the Divine, which is expressed when a Spirit inhabits a human body. We also experience this Perfect and Divine Circle when we consummate a loving relationship, expressing the Spirit's pure love in a physical way, binding the two realms.

"No, the body is not merely a vessel for the Spirit. They are symbiotically connected. There are times when the Spirit is too deeply injured, and the Life Force is not sufficient to carry on. The physical body cannot maintain wholeness and integrity when it houses a deeply wounded Spirit. It is entirely affected by the Spirit, and will manifest all that Spirit is."

Once again, the Spirit paused, deep in thought for a time, reflecting on how it came to be that she learned this Lesson. The Old Man, the God and the Goddess waited patiently until she was ready to continue.

"Further, as with most problems and obstacles of an Earthly Life, they are just more Lessons that the Spirit is learning through Human experience, and therefore, they can only be overcome by Spiritual means. So often, Humans look outside themselves for answers. They seek to blame someone for their difficulties and frailties, rather than looking inside, which will direct them to the Heavens, and which will then lead them back to the Divine, the Higher Purpose, the Reason For All Things. As difficult as their lives can be, it must be so in order for them to learn the Lessons that they chose. And so it was in the families I selected. I knew what it would be when I made the decision, and you knew it when I sought your approval for this Life. But as you know, we no longer remember those choices once we are there, and stumble along until some part of our Spirit shines through to remind us of the Divine. Then the real Learning begins, the Learning of the Spirit, the reason for the whole experience at all.

"I had many very hard lessons to learn with these families, and as painful and difficult as the experience was, I am grateful for all of it, for it was an excellent opportunity to learn those Lessons which I finally did complete. But I also entered these families as a teacher, and found that they did not wish to learn. It is such a complicated process, isn't it, how we all choose our Human Lives to work out our Spiritual Lessons, and the choice is made in an interconnected, intertwining way, involving many others. We all begin our Human Lives, knowing full well what we will encounter, and who will be in our Lives, and what we are meant to learn while there. It appears to Humans as though some people waste a Life, seeming to refuse to learn while they are there; yet that is all a valuable part of the Greater Plan. It is meant to be exactly the way it is."

She paused, reflecting. "There is just so much to tell; there were far more Lessons in this Life than I could begin to relate to you. I have told you some of the most important ones, the ones that were truly Life-Altering for me, and ultimately, Soul-Saving as well, but there are more that I must share with you.

"After years of pain and difficulty, and searching for something without knowing what it was, I realized that I had been wasting valuable time and energy, trying to find a Human being to fix my need for love and belonging, until I finally understood that this was a Spiritual Lesson, which began when I was unwanted at conception. I tolerated abuse and unhappiness in the name of love until I finally understood that no Human being could, or even should attempt to fix my Spiritual issues for me.

"I realized that as a Spiritual Being, I needed to reconnect with the Source of all Love, my true Parents, my true Creators, God and Goddess, and that was how I could find healing and Perfect Love. One of the most powerful Lessons in reconnecting with my Creators was to understand that I had always been Loved, even when I did not feel it because of all the Human conditions surrounding me. Nor had I ever been alone, yet I had felt that way all of my Life until that point.

"After that day, I spent a fair amount of time, casting Sacred Circles in which I remembered and visited with my true Parents, allowing myself to feel their love, and their comforting. Each time, it was a bittersweet reunion, having been away so long, but also being very happy to be back in the embrace of those who knew me, accepted me, and loved me completely, for all I was, and despite all I was not.

"From that point on, I was much more able to remember my Spirit and to honour it. I had been trying to live a more Spiritual lifestyle before that time, but there were dramatic changes after that. I looked at everything differently, and especially, all my relationships. I saw how so many Human frailties make themselves evident in them, and how it is very difficult to have a truly loving and nurturing relationship of any kind with anyone, when there is no Spiritual basis for it.

"I learned that I let others strip me of my confidence because of their opinions of me. It took years of pain and heartache to understand that this is a Human issue with many Spiritual Lessons attached. One of these has to do with judgement, and understanding that although as Human beings, we sometimes tend to fall into this behaviour, it is another Lesson for the Spirit to realize that it comes from a lack of Spiritual awareness and growth. Allowing myself to be affected by someone in that state was only Self-destructive; it served no useful purpose. Another's opinion is not necessarily based in fact, yet as Humans, we tend to forget that, and make decisions about ourselves and the world around us, simply based on what another person thinks. We do not honour the Spirit when we make such choices; rather, we destroy it.

"In this Life, I had what felt like more than enough Lessons to do with Self-destruction; that was one which I was happy to recognize and release when it came to me. Judgement comes from insecurities and other wounds. There is no place for such behaviour in a relationship that is based in Divinely Inspired Spirit. It makes no sense to Self-destruct over someone else's refusal to learn Spiritual Lessons. There comes a time when we must realize that our belief system was created largely by other's opinions of us as we are growing up, and that we will continually seek out people who will validate these beliefs after we have become adults.

"But it is only a belief system, and the beliefs are fed to us because they came from another. Worse than that, it does not even have to be someone we know, love, or trust. That belief system is not necessarily based in fact, and is open to a complete re-evaluation, throwing out the toxic beliefs that are invalid, and rebuilding our beliefs based on facts and ideals. Only then can we live in Truth as our Higher Selves."

Spirit was lost in thought for a while after this, then finally, she spoke once more. "Another of the most important Lessons I learned in this Life was that we must recognize that we have no control over what someone else's thoughts might be. It does not matter who we are or what we do, ultimately another person's opinion is his or her own business and we cannot control it, though we often try, or even take responsibility for it.

"As well, the moment we allow other people's opinions, or even our fear of their opinions, to influence any choices we make, or how we feel about ourselves, we have given them our power and our control, even if they are unaware of it, even if they did not ask for it, even if they never abuse it. We have given up ourselves, and are then operating from a position of fear, doubt and insecurity. Coming from such a place, it is impossible to function at our best, or be our Highest Selves.

"And the worst of this is that it is of our own making; if we allow this, we are not in a place of self-love or self-respect, because in doing so, we have handed over our Selves to this person, and again, even if that person is unaware. It is the ultimate in giving up control when we do it without someone else even attempting to take it.

"This issue raises another. Much earlier in this Life, I had learned that there is no room for control in any relationship, other than self-control. I had become quite good at functioning without being controlling, at least, not in the usual unhealthy ways about which I had learned. But at this particular point in my journey, when I was digging deeply into myself in my search for understanding and Spiritual growth, I also saw a very subtle, yet powerful form of control in relationships, which I had never seen before, and which completely surprised me.

"This kind of control is seen when Humans are restrictive of another person, under the guise of being concerned about his or her health and well-being. If a husband, for example, is being restricted by his wife in terms of what he may or may not eat, drink, or otherwise ingest, she may insist that it is because she is worried about him, which, in her mind, may well be the case. However, it is still his choice, his Karma, his Lessons which ultimately end up being affected. It is not love in its highest and purest form. In fact, it is not based in love at all. It is based in fear.

"And although it looks relatively innocuous, and can even appear to be helpful and loving behaviour, it is actually quite destructive. When we inhabit Human bodies, we do tend to live a very Human experience. After all, that is the point, of course. It can become difficult to find or remember the Spiritual Path, and because it is sometimes less demanding to live in the Humanness than in our Highest Selves, it can be very easy to slip into Human ways of thinking, behaving and connecting.

"In that example, it is easy for the wife to say she loves her husband and does not want him to die because he did not take care of himself. And it is easy for him to go along with it to please her, or because he is afraid to die. Or maybe he goes along with it out of respect for her because he loves her.

"But think about his Karmic Lessons in any of those responses to her insistence that he live according to her rules for his good health. If he goes along with them to please her, there is an obvious Karmic Lesson he is missing in making that decision. Why does he need to please her? That is going to be a Spiritual Lesson, and he is missing the opportunity to learn it. Or what if it is because he is afraid to die? The answer is the same. And as well, if he does it because he loves her, then once again, he is missing the Karmic Lesson.

"If he is going to do it at all, it should be because he is doing it for himself, out of respect for his own body, his own health and well-being, and of course, only he should be worrying about his Spiritual Lessons, for only he can recognize and master them.

"It does not matter what the reason for the wife's behaviour may be; the fact remains that in this example, the husband is being asked to change. Whether the wife truly believes that it is for his own good, and it is out of love for him, it is about her need to have some control over him to alleviate her own fears or needs. There is nothing selfless in it at all, not really. It is about her wanting to be with him, being afraid to lose him, being afraid of his death, or afraid of being on her own, or any number of other things. But none of the wife's actions or the husband's responses are about love. They are entirely about issues with fear and control. So ultimately, not only is she interfering with his Karmic Lessons, she is missing the opportunity to master some of her own as well.

"Interestingly, as Spirits, we love to change. We love to learn. It is part of our purpose! Yet when we take Human form, the point of which is to allow us that learning, we become terrified of change, terrified of growth. And worse, as Humans, none of us wants to be told to change to please someone else, yet we think nothing of expecting someone else to change to suit us. That is a huge injustice to all concerned. It is an injustice on the most basic level of Human love and respect, but it is a much larger injustice on the Spiritual and Karmic levels."

There was a pensive look across the sensitive face for a few moments before the Spirit continued.

"One of my favourite Life-Altering, Soul-Saving Lessons came not long after that one. I was continuing my deepening self-discovery and awareness, and had come up against a particularly horrible time in that Life. Since I could not remember my choices from this side, I had begun to question my Karmic Lessons and my Destiny. I had begun to wonder whether I was destined only to struggle, because it seemed that no matter how I worked to try to make things better, I kept ending up in the same lonely, unhappy place. I believed that everything happens exactly the way it is meant to do; therefore, I began to think that it did not matter what I did, I was not supposed to be happy.

"I had also always believed that there was still room for Free Will and Choice, though at that point, I had not got very far in trying to figure out how they fit with Things Meant To Be. I felt the need to begin a fairly lengthy Self-analysis. Not like the ones we do here, of course, but I made my first reasonable attempt at it for that Life, and I was really quite surprised by the answers that came to me.

"As I examined the major turning points in that Life, I tore apart each choice. I was quite ruthless about it, because I knew I would get nowhere if I could not be completely honest with myself. I was determined to understand why I had made the major choices that had significantly altered the course of my Life. Eventually, I saw a common thread running through each choice, and although it should not really have shocked me, for some reason, it did.

"What I saw was fear. It was the driving force behind every major choice I had made until that time. And even worse, in most of those cases, I was well aware of it being there, prompting my choice. I really did not understand what that meant on each of those occasions, or what it would come to mean in the course of my Life.

"I went one step further in my efforts to understand on the deepest possible level what had been taking place in my Life, or at least, the deepest that I was meant to go at that point. When I examined the fear, I saw that it went back to my first human consciousness in that Life, at the moment of my conception, the fear for my survival because I was unwanted and unloved. That Lesson was repeated over and over again during that Life, and it was not until that experience of self-analysis that I became aware of how profoundly and negatively that fear had affected me."

She stopped for a few moments, and it seemed as though she were replaying some of these events in her mind. A sweet, sorrowful expression appeared briefly on her face, while she paused to consider her own words.

She continued, "I realized once again that I had been misguided in my efforts to stop feeling fear. Of course, in reality, I was only running from it. In fact, it seemed to grow, the fear feeding itself, taking on a life of its own. It seemed the more I tried to hide from it, the more fearful situations presented themselves.

"Foolishly, I did not understand that to avoid them did not mean I could avoid the Fear, itself. It followed me everywhere for my entire Life until that time, and with some horror, I realized that I had given it much of my Life. Finally, I decided to stop running. I turned around, planted my feet firmly in the ground and looked Fear in the eye. I challenged it. I wanted -- no, I *demanded* that it give my Life back. I will not pretend that I did not still experience Fear after this; however, I refused to allow it any more power. I refused to give it any more of my Life."

The three listeners were intrigued. They smiled as they felt the strength that Spirit had gained with this Lesson, strength that was no longer Self-destructive, strength that was about beginning to achieve Wholeness and Healing. They remembered well what she had written about this extremely difficult Lesson when she applied for this particular Life. They knew how important this was, what it meant to this Spirit.

She continued. "Once I stopped letting Fear stop me, my Life was completely different. I was overwhelmed by how many facets of it changed for the better.   It was as though someone had handed me an entirely new Life. I took risks in relationships, daring to speak my Truth, despite the possible consequences. I no longer feared my vulnerability, and was able to shed my Self-destructive image of infallible strength.   There was great healing just in that alone. I tried countless things that I would never have dared try before, putting myself in what I perceived to be terrifying situations which usually proved to be absolutely simple or exhilarating, exciting, or joyful. It was the first taste of real freedom I had in this Life. Indeed, it was very empowering."

With a far-away look in her eyes, a peaceful expression crossed the Spirit's face, and a gentle little smile followed. She was quiet for a few moments, remembering the releasing of Fear.

"My hard-fought battle with Fear led me to a clearer vision of another Lesson which had been evident throughout my Life. This was the Lesson of Letting Go. Until that time, I had thought of them as separate. But in time, I reached a point where I saw them as connected. I was very small when I understood that I was going to have to let go of a lot in my Life, and rather than accept this, I fought hard to hold on, out of a deep need for security, stability, and of course, love. To let go was terrifying. I held on to material things, to beliefs, to relationships, to anything which seemed to fill a part of the deep yearning and longing which I had always felt.

"To learn this Lesson meant facing my Fear of Letting Go. It meant recognizing and letting go of the Self-destructive behaviours and the Human needs that were driving them. It meant one of the longest climbs to connecting with my Highest Self, and of course, as you are well aware, was one of the times I relied most heavily on you, my Divine

Creators. I could feel your Love and Strength very powerfully during those days, reminding me that as long as I walked Your Path, the journey would not be as arduous as I feared.

"There were many occasions in my Life which offered me the opportunity to learn about Letting Go, so it was not an unfamiliar companion. The difference on this occasion, when I could see that it was connected to Fear, was that I was forced to examine it and learn it in a much deeper fashion.

"I thought about the substantial amount of time I had spent, unable to let go of the Past and how long I had wished to change it. How long I had dreamed of reliving previous experiences, in the hopes of putting them right. I wasted so much time looking behind me, revisiting where I had already been, that often, I did not notice the path I was on, much less the road ahead. In doing this, I missed much of my Life, and in that moment of realization, I was given yet another opportunity to stop wasting any more of it. What a blessing!"

The Spirit paused for a very long time at this point, reflecting most thoughtfully. The three listeners sat patiently in silence, allowing her the time she needed before she carried on.

"Once again, I was struck by the way the Lessons fit together, for as I began work in earnest, learning to let go, I came face to face with one Lesson which I had been avoiding for a very long time. It was the Lesson of Forgiveness. I felt its sting, like alcohol in an open wound, raw and burning every time it crossed my mind. I had been hurt by two people on such a profoundly deep Spiritual level that I did not think I could ever heal, and I was certain I would never forgive them. I needed to hang on to the hatred and the anger for more than one reason. In part, I believed it would be a betrayal of my Self if I were to forgive them. But there was more -- more that I did not wish to see.

"Although I was well aware that I was the only one being hurt by my unforgiving heart, I felt justified in holding onto the anger, and I did not care if it was hurting me. It seemed right and necessary for me to do it, and it took a long time before I understood that these men would never understand how they had affected me, nor was it likely that they would ever care. I understood that in all likelihood, they probably gave me very little thought at all. Meanwhile, I was filled with toxic, destructive hatred and anger for these people, refusing to forgive them for what I perceived were their sins against me, not wanting to accept that I was doing myself far more harm than they had ever done to me.

"It was another enormous gift of Freedom for myself, when I was finally able to release the hatred and the anger that I held in my heart, and to replace it with forgiveness. Though they were unaware, it was also a gift to them, because until that day, my Spirit was creating negative energy that was sent to them without my notice. Once I learned this aspect of Forgiveness, and the energy became more positive, it could only do good things for them, and for me.

"It took me a very long time to accept that the situations with these people were also Spiritual Lessons, and to accept that they were Meant To Be, that I had chosen them before I requested this Life, and that everyone involved was doing exactly as they were supposed to do. It was all a part of the Greater Plan. All those concerned had Lessons to learn; everything was connected. My anger was futile, its only result was destructive to all concerned, as there was no Human resolution ever possible in either of those situations. Rather, they required Spiritual resolution, because they were designed to be a part of our Spiritual learning.

"I saw how I had been hurting my Self, both on the physical level and in the Spiritual realm, as well. I was creating a toxic environment for my body, and I was not allowing my Spirit to be free to grow and learn. I had put my Self in chains. And directing negative energy at these people was also keeping them in chains, which was not only detrimental to my own progress, but to theirs as well. I finally understood that I had to let it all go. We all had Lessons to learn. I had no right to prevent or interfere with that. It was when I saw my refusal to 'let go' and forgive that I saw the connection between these two valuable Lessons.

"I feel I must add that the Mother was not one of those whom I hated, for I knew that she was one of my most important teachers, and because of her, I was given the opportunity to learn some of my greatest Lessons, which ultimately enriched my Life and helped me to fulfill my purpose on Earth. I struggled for a long time, however, until I reached this place of understanding, which included understanding that she, too, was a very wounded Soul.

"We were, in fact, quite similar in one respect; each of us had hurt the other, as a result of the injuries to our own Spirits. For years after I realized this, I longed to have this conversation with her, and to tell her of my learning, and of my love and appreciation for her as a Spiritual being, despite the great pain I had felt as her Human Daughter. I wanted to tell her that although I had not intended it, I had also caused her pain during my Life, and to ask her Forgiveness, and to explain all of this to her.

"However, I knew she was a very Young Spirit. It was

another occasion for me to let go of my Earthly needs, and to remember my Spiritual Lessons. I was well aware that she had not progressed enough in her own learning to be able to hear or appreciate my words. But she will now."

And far away, the Mother's crystal star suddenly began to shine more brightly, as very many of its scars were healed due to the appreciation, understanding, forgiveness and love of the Daughter.

"What I also came to realize," she continued, "was that there are two other aspects of Forgiveness that are vital to our happiness and our well-being, to our healing. We must also learn to ask forgiveness when we have hurt others, because if we have caused pain, it is essential to their healing to know that we understand what we did, and it is essential to our own growth, as we realize where we went wrong, and so we may do our best to avoid causing hurt again.

"In all of the Lessons to do with Forgiveness, I found that the hardest one was to forgive myself. No one was harder on me than I. No one could have made me feel more remorse for my mistakes than I. And even when others had forgiven me, even when I had not gone nearly as wrong as I had thought, I still struggled with forgiving myself. It took many long years before I could do this, always having expected perfection from myself, but from no one else, even though I knew I could not master it. And when I did not live up to my expectations of myself, when I felt I had failed myself or others, I thought that not only were my actions unforgivable, but I was, as well. In trying to understand why I felt that way, it eventually became evident to me that Forgiveness of Self became wrapped up in my first conscious moment as a human; I was not worthy of living or of being loved.

"As I contemplated the Lessons I had learned regarding Fear, Letting Go, and Forgiveness, and having been led back to my earliest pain in this human Life, I saw very clearly another Lesson which had been trying to surface for some time. Although I had managed a small amount of progress with it in some areas of my Life, I could see at this juncture that it was of a magnitude that I found to be overwhelming. I had been struggling with the Lesson of Acceptance throughout my life, with each fearful moment, with each occasion of having to let go of someone or something I loved. I believed that all conditions of life serve a Higher Purpose, yet I had not managed total Acceptance of this idea.

"As I tried to understand what was creating this obstacle, my eyes were opened to another facet of the Lesson of Fear. As I have described to you, once I saw how much I had let Fear control my Life, I refused to allow this any longer. I began making choices, in spite of Fear, rather than because of it. I learned that having courage does not mean being Fearless, but rather, it means having the Fear and facing it, rather than attempting to run or hide from it.

"But once I reached the Lesson of Acceptance, and searched inside my Self to determine why I seemed unable to master it, I saw that I had only learned the Lesson of Facing Fear in terms of situations over which I had some control. It was in decisions and choices that I had come to believe I had mastered it. In this way, I had conquered and released many fears, or when I still felt it, I refused to allow it to be part of my decision-making process.

"However, I suddenly realized that I still felt an enormous amount of Fear about situations over which I had no control. I feared that my husband would die. I feared that I would develop a terrible illness and be subjected to great pain and suffering. I feared for the long-term safety and well-being of my Self and the people I loved.

"It was then that I realized what was holding me back, and I saw once again how these pieces of the puzzle fit together. I could not control these things, so they frightened me. And this Fear led me back to the Lesson of Letting Go, and I saw in yet another way how I needed to reinforce that Lesson. Suddenly, I saw one of the most important Lessons that until that point, I had not yet fully understood. It was vital to all the others. It played a significant part in the unfolding and piecing together of a Lifetime of learning. I had neglected a monumental part of the entire picture. It was in the Lesson of Trust."

Spirit paused for a moment, having grown rather serious, and was quiet. Her listeners were intrigued, wanting to hear more, but allowing the silence.

"For most of this Life, I had trusted in people and Earthly situations entirely too much. Repeatedly, my trust was betrayed, and I ended up deeply wounded because of it, but it was because of my Human need to be loved that I freely gave my trust to anyone who would have it, and many who did not deserve it. I was considering how I had always been a very trusting person, and thought I had mastered that particular Lesson, so I was struggling to understand how it fit with the rest of my learning, especially with regard to the issue of Acceptance.

"And that is when the lightning bolt hit! My trust had been entirely misplaced! How could I have so freely trusted in imperfect Humans and in Earthly situations created by them, while at the same time, have difficulty placing trust in God and Goddess, in their Divine Wisdom and Grace, and in the Greater Plan? I truly believed that all conditions of life served a Higher Purpose, so why did I struggle with trusting the Divine Creators of All Things?

"I was overwhelmed by the power in that thought, and by its simplicity as well. It may have been that until that time, the little child deep in my Soul was remembering all the parents who abandoned her in one form or another, creating my ability to trust only in relationships over which I had some measure of control. My attachments to my True Parents had been broken for many years, then limped along as I worked at healing them. It was not until those attachments had become strong and clear that I recognized that they had always been, and would always be here to support me and to love me through whatever lay ahead. After a misguided and lifelong search, I had finally found Perfect Trust.

"Along with this came an even greater release and Letting Go, as I felt all those related issues begin to crumble and dissipate. No longer did I have room for even the smallest measure of trying to control what was out of my hands. So many fears and Human needs just melted away, as I remembered Perfect Trust.

"And as these pieces of the puzzle came together, I saw another, quietly moving in and taking its rightful place amongst the rest."

Spirit's eyes danced, and she smiled a wide and peaceful smile that warmed the hearts of those in her company. Eager to share more, she excitedly went on.

"Having finally understood the Lesson of Perfect Trust, I was suddenly struck by the realization that Letting Go and Trusting in the Greater Plan must naturally lead to the Lesson of Acceptance. Once again, I was amazed by simplicity in this. The feeling of Freedom that washed over me in that moment was incredibly powerful and Life-Giving! I will never forget it.

"In that moment, I understood that Perfect Trust resulted in Perfect Acceptance of What Was Meant To Be, which included all conditions of Life. I did, however, discover that the Lesson of Acceptance was not quite so simple, in and of itself, for it carried with it more than just one part. Although I had long before learned Acceptance of others, I had continually struggled with the hardest of all, Acceptance of Self. But then, the answer came to me. I knew what had been missing, what made accepting my Self so difficult. It was impossible without Perfect Love.

"I will not forget the clarity with which I suddenly saw so many Lessons fall into place at one time! It was truly a defining moment in my Life, years' worth of difficult struggle and trying to make sense of so many disjointed parts and Lessons, and all of it was right there before me, one leading to the next, which led to the next...I could not believe I had been unable to see it all before; it was just too simple! There they were, Perfect Love, Perfect Trust, and Perfect Acceptance, each requiring the others; a Divine Trinity, all that we really need."

Spirit smiled, and slowly shook her head from side to side, seeming to gently chide herself for having taken so long to recognize this.

After a few moments, she shifted her focus from remembering that moment, and she continued, eager to further explain.

"My healing journey was, of course, very long, and happened in little pieces at a time. I had been taking my Life apart and examining it closely, trying to understand it and improve it. Of course, one of the most difficult struggles I had was with relationships with partners. I had made much progress in healing the spiritual issues that had arisen in that area, and finally I met a man who seemed too good to be true. Over and over again, he showed me unconditional love. Never did he judge or criticize. He always supported and encouraged me, and everything I needed to do, or was meant to be.

"He was patient and truly cared about me, and respected me. He did not have to agree with my thoughts or my deeds, but they were always accepted by him, as was I. He had the purest heart and soul of anyone I had ever met. He showed me as perfect a love, and as perfect a trust as any Human being ever could. This man only seemed to know how to live in his Highest Self. He was truly very directly connected with his Divine Spirit.

"I left the Spirit World and began my Human experience, in which I was meant to learn about Perfect Love, Perfect Trust, and Perfect Acceptance. From the beginning of my Human Life, I believed these did not exist in my world. But through the course of my Life and my learning, I came to understand that I had always had them from You, my Beloved Parents. And because of your pure and abiding love for me, I was able to experience a relationship which was based on the example of yours. This beautiful marriage was a very powerful expression of the Divine, of everything to which we should aspire during our Human Lives. I saw, in our marriage, a Human reflection of You, Beloved God and Goddess, and your Perfect Love, Trust and Acceptance. I had ended where I had begun: from the Spirit Realm, to the Earthly Life, and back again, a perfect demonstration of Spiritual Being having Human experience; the Spiritual Realm on Earth. I had found my way Home."

Once more, Spirit wore a far-away expression, and her eyes grew misty as she remembered her husband, and recalled their parting. It was something she could not begin to describe. She had so cherished their time together; his great love for her could be felt, even had he never spoken a word of it. It was as pure and perfect a love and a union as she could have ever imagined.

She knew that she was gradually moving away from her Earthly connections, and these were the last Human thoughts she would have of her sweet husband. And although she knew she would always remember him in the Spirit World, it would never be in the same way as she did now, while still in touch with the Earthly Realm. Therefore, she chose to keep sacred and private, her last thoughts as his wife.

It was a pensive Spirit who paced back and forth, a few slow steps, considering what next to say. It seemed to the listeners that she was about to make her summation. They waited patiently for her to begin to speak once again.

"Even when the Human element is strongly connected with the Spirit, the Lessons feel so hard on the Other Side. Before we are Master Spirits, we will tell each other as Humans that we would not appreciate the good parts of Life without the bad. But that is only because all the Lessons have not yet been learned. On this side, we know what it will be someday, but they cannot yet understand. Only when we have mastered all the Lessons that God and Goddess have to teach us, and when we are filled with Divine Wisdom and Love, will there be a deep appreciation for the Earthly Life in its perfect state, that imperfect Humans cannot grasp.

"But it really is just so simple, all of it. If only they knew...I long for the day when all Human suffering and frailty will be gone. The symbiotic relationship between Spirit and Human will be a dance of Perfection. With no more Spiritual wounds, there will be no disease or illness of body, mind or emotions. When the Earthly Life is done, there will be a simple and painless shedding of the Human body. Spirits will continue to choose New Lives, but not for the purpose of Learning. It will be for the purpose of enjoying the fruits of their labours in previous Lives while they were completing the Wheel of Learning. With all Human life being expressed in the perfection of Master Spirits, the world will be a Paradise like nothing ever imagined by people before. All Spirits will have finally learned all possible Lessons, and will live as Humans in their Highest Selves, creating Heaven on Earth, with complete Peace and Tranquility, and in the Purest Love."

The Creators and the Old Man were beaming. Clearly, many Lessons had been learned, and this Spirit was going to be ready for many more difficult challenges in the future. They were happy to have her back Home, and were very pleased for her regarding her significant accomplishments.

The time had come to accompany her Creators and the Old Man to her crystal star, the Mirror of her Soul, where she would remain, pondering the Lessons she had learned in this Life, waiting until it was time for her next. As the group drifted through the Heavens, Spirit lost all resemblance to her most recent Human form. Upon reaching the crystal, there was only the True Self in all its purity.

The Goddess looked lovingly at Spirit and said, "You have done well with your Lessons. Go now and be a source of Light and Inspiration for the other Spirits, as you ponder your learnings, your teachings, and as you prepare for yet another Life in the future."

God and Goddess embraced Spirit, as did the Keeper of the Stars. Spirit then stood in front of the large crystal, as she had done so long ago at the beginning of the Life she just completed. She faced the others, holding her arms out to them in love, and quietly glowing. Turning back toward the star, she began to swirl around it, slowly at first, then faster and faster, gradually shining brighter in the night sky. The cracks, scratches, and scrapes began to vanish almost instantly, restoring the great crystal, as her radiant energy once again engulfed the beautiful star. It was in this that Spirit's Lessons were most evident, for it was in the Lessons learned, and in the forgiveness for which she had asked, and which she had been shown, that the healing took place.

Suddenly, with a flash that illuminated the Heavens, she was inside the crystal, shining brilliantly in the night sky. And as her essence radiated across the Heavens, the dimly-lit stars of the Spirits who had so wounded her, all began to shine a little more brightly, as her forgiveness of them healed the damage they had done to their own crystals. Those Spirits all knew that this act of forgiveness, in all its simplicity, yet complexity, had just taught them a Lesson that they would take with them into their next Lives. They were humbled by it, and would not soon forget it.

And now, when you look up into a clear night sky, you can search among the very brightest stars, and know that it is one of these that is this gentle and loving Spirit, pondering Lessons learned, still teaching other Spirits through her radiance, yet still a student, contemplating the challenges and Lessons to come.

Printed in the United Kingdom
by Lightning Source UK Ltd.
105705UKS00001B/19-42